W9-DBA-368

Brandon escorted Sonya to her car, his nerves alert, senses sharp.

She started to slide in the driver's seat when he noticed a small square of paper about the size of an index card under her windshield wiper. "What's this?"

He handed it to her and leaned in to read along with her. "Stop looking for Heather Bradley. She doesn't want to be found."

Sonya gaped. The baby kidnapped twenty-eight years ago. "Well, I guess we're making someone kind of nervous."

A muscle jumped in his jaw as he stared at the note.

"So what do we do?" she asked.

Brandon lifted a brow. "Do you want to stop looking for her?"

"No way."

She glanced around the parking lot, wondering if the person who'd left the note was watching. Shivers slid up and down her spine.

Spooked, she stayed close to the person who seemed to represent the only security she could find in a world that had shifted on its axis once again. First the death of her father, then her mother. Now someone was sending her threats.

Books by Lynette Eason

Love Inspired Suspense

LYNETTE EASON

makes her home in South Carolina with her husband and two children. Lynette has taught in many areas of education over the past ten years and is very happy to make the transition from teaching school to teaching at writers' conferences. She is a member of RWA (Romance Writers of America), FHL (Faith, Hope, & Love) and ACFW (American Christian Fiction Writers). She is often found online and loves to talk writing with anyone who will listen. You can find her at www.facebook.com/lynetteeasonauthor or www.lynetteeason.com.

HER STOLEN PAST

LYNETTE EASON

HARLEQUIN® LOVE INSPIRED® SUSPENSE

If you purchased this book without a cover you should be aware
that this book is stolen property. It was reported as "unsold and
destroyed" to the publisher, and neither the author nor the
publisher has received any payment for this "stripped book."

Recycling programs
for this product may
not exist in your area.

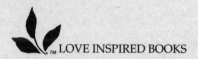

™ LOVE INSPIRED BOOKS

ISBN-13: 978-0-373-67623-1

HER STOLEN PAST

Copyright © 2014 by Lynette Eason

All rights reserved. Except for use in any review, the reproduction
or utilization of this work in whole or in part in any form by any
electronic, mechanical or other means, now known or hereinafter
invented, including xerography, photocopying and recording, or in
any information storage or retrieval system, is forbidden without
the written permission of the editorial office, Love Inspired Books,
233 Broadway, New York, NY 10279 U.S.A.

This is a work of fiction. Names, characters, places and incidents are
either the product of the author's imagination or are used fictitiously, and
any resemblance to actual persons, living or dead, business establishments,
events or locales is entirely coincidental.

This edition published by arrangement with Love Inspired Books.

® and TM are trademarks of Love Inspired Books, used under license.
Trademarks indicated with ® are registered in the United States Patent
and Trademark Office, the Canadian Intellectual Property Office and in
other countries.

www.Harlequin.com

Printed in U.S.A.

Repent, then, and turn to God, so that your sins
may be wiped out, that times of refreshing
may come from the Lord.
—*Acts* 3:19

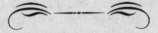

To my wonderful, crazy family.
I love y'all so much. I couldn't do this without you.
Thank you for being willing to put up with
my deadline frenzies and take-out food.

To my awesome editor, Emily Rodmell.
It's been a while since I said thanks in a dedication,
so here you go. Thank you for pulling me out
of the slush pile back in 2007 and giving me
a shot at my dreams. :-)

To my Lord and Savior, Jesus Christ.
I love you more every day. Thank you for my gift
of writing. Thank you for letting me do it for you.
May you continue to bless me with stories
and ideas so I can reach others for you.

ONE

Sonya Daniels heard the sharp crack and saw the woman jogging four feet in front of her stumble. Then fall.

Another crack.

Another woman cried out and hit the ground.

"Shooter! Get down! Get down!"

With a burst of horror, Sonya caught on. Someone was shooting at the joggers on the path. Terror froze her for a brief second. A second that saved her life as the bullet whizzed past her head and planted itself in the wooden bench next to her. If she'd been moving forward, she would be dead.

Frantic, she registered the screams of those in the park as she ran full out, zigzagging her way to the concrete fountain just ahead.

Her only thought was shelter.

A bullet slammed into the dirt behind her and she dropped to roll next to the base of the fountain.

She looked up to find another young woman had beaten her there. Terrified brown eyes stared at Sonya and she knew the woman saw her fear reflected back at her. Panting, Sonya listened for more shots.

None came.

And still they waited. Seconds turned into minutes.

"Is it over?" the woman finally whispered. "Is he gone?"

"I don't know," Sonya responded. "Let's just stay here for a while longer."

Screams still echoed around them. Wails and petrified cries of disbelief.

Sonya lifted her head slightly and looked back at the two women who'd fallen. They still lay on the path behind her. *Oh, Lord, help me help them.* She reached for her cell phone. Had anyone called 911? Surely they had, but one more call wouldn't hurt.

Her trembling fingers refused to hold the device and it fell to the ground in front of her. She curled her hands into fists, desperate to control the shaking. She'd done this before. She could manage the fear. But never before had she been caught by surprise like this.

Sirens sounded.

Sonya grabbed her phone and shoved it into the armband she wore when running. She took a deep breath and scanned the area across the street. She'd been in dangerous situations before, working the streets first as a paramedic, then as a trauma nurse on an air-ambulance helicopter.

Later, she'd shake her head at the irony. All those times she'd been in the midst of the flying bullets and had come out unscathed. Now she was a hospice nurse on her day off and she got shot at. Slowly, she calmed and gained control of her pounding pulse.

Her mind clicked through the shots fired. Two hit the women running in front of her. Her stomach cramped at the thought that she should have been the third victim. She glanced at the bench. The bullet hole stared back. It had dug a groove, slanted and angled. He was shooting down, which meant he was higher up.

She had no idea which building the shots came from, but if she had to guess, she would pick the one directly across the street. The office building? Or the clothing warehouse?

The police would figure it out. She checked her watch. No more shots had sounded in the few minutes she'd lain next to the cement fountain, her mind spinning. There were wounded people who needed her.

Heart in her throat, Sonya darted to the nearest woman, who lay about ten yards away from her. Expecting a bullet to slam into her at any moment, she felt for a pulse.

* * *

Brandon Hayes heard the gunfire through the open window of his third-floor part-time office at Finding the Lost and automatically reached for his weapon as he spun in his chair.

A police detective by profession and a Finding the Lost employee on his days off, he didn't have a lot of downtime. Nor did he want any.

The Glock felt natural and comfortable in his right hand. He stepped to the side of the window and looked out.

Chaos reigned in the park below.

Two people lay on the ground and appeared to be injured.

Erica James, his sister and founder of Finding the Lost, bolted into the office. "What was that?"

"Bullets. There's a shooter nearby and people are hurt."

She pulled out her cell phone. "Someone's probably already called, but—"

Brandon heard her reporting the incident to the 911 operator as he tried to pinpoint the location where the bullets originated from.

His gaze shifted from the horror below him to the building beside him. Nothing. Not a flash, no movement, nothing. He grabbed the phone from his desk. Rachel, his cousin and secretary for Finding the Lost, picked up. "Get this building locked down now."

"I already did. I heard you say something about bullets fired and immediately called security."

"Good." Her office was just outside of his.

He returned to the window and watched the craziness unfold in the park, assessing the situation, planning the best way to help. Go after the shooter or help the victims?

Movement by the fountain caught his eye. A woman trying to pull one of the injured ones to safety.

Wait a minute.

"Hey, isn't that Sonya Daniels? What's she trying to do? Get herself killed?" He raced from the office, Erica's protests ringing in his ears. "Stay here!"

Brandon hit the glass door, swiped his card that would allow him to exit, but would lock the door behind him. Then he was on the sidewalk. Within seconds he was at the park. Police officers who'd been nearby started to arrive on the scene. To the nearest one, Brandon flashed his badge and yelled, "I think the shooter was in the building next to the bank."

Law enforcement now swarmed the area and he kept his badge in plain sight. He stuck his weapon back in the shoulder holster and headed for the fountain. Sonya Daniels had shown up at Finding the Lost a little over a week ago with a birth certificate for Heather Bradley. She'd hired him to find the person. And now she was rescuing joggers in the park. His heart thudded as he kept his attention tuned to the area around him.

No more shots sounded. He hoped that meant the shooter was on the run and not aiming at any more innocent people.

Brandon rounded the back of the fountain and found Sonya doing CPR on the woman she'd pulled out of harm's way. He dropped beside her. "What can I do?"

Surprise and relief flickered across her face when she saw him. "She needs an ambulance. Her heart's stopped." Sonya did more compressions. "Feel for a pulse."

Brandon did as ordered. He looked up and shook his head.

Sonya gave a growl of frustration and slammed a fist onto the woman's chest. "Beat!" She pressed and released, pressed and released, unrelenting and breathless, with determination etched on her features.

Brandon felt a faint flutter under his fingers. "Keep going. I think I felt something."

Hope blazed in her eyes as she continued her efforts. "Come on, please. Please." An ambulance pulled up next to the fountain and two paramedics rushed over. Sonya looked up. "I think she has a pulse now. She coded about thirty seconds ago."

"You have medical training?" the first paramedic asked as she dropped beside Sonya.

"Yes. One semester short of being a doctor."

Brandon shot her a look. He hadn't known that.

He moved aside as the other paramedic joined them. Sonya fell back out of the way and let them take over. He grasped her arm. More medical help surrounded the other woman. "She's dead," Sonya whispered to him. "The bullet went straight through her head." Grief coated her words. "The one I was helping was shot in the back. Please let her make it, God." Brandon wondered if she even realized she'd whispered her prayer aloud. He hoped God listened to her more than He seemed to hear Brandon's prayers.

He watched the officers doing their job and knew Sonya needed to give a statement, but for now, he needed to get her someplace where she could sit and let the adrenaline ebb. He cupped her elbow and started to lead her away. She resisted. "No, I want to watch them."

Finally, one of the EMTs looked up, caught Sonya's eye and nodded. They moved the woman to the gurney and slid her in the back of the ambulance. The female paramedic looked back and gave a thumbs-up.

Sonya blew out a breath and leaned back against the bench.

An officer approached them. "Has anyone talked to you two yet?"

"No," Brandon said. "I heard the shots from my office window across the street and ran over to see if I could help."

Sonya looked up, then pointed to the hole in the bench. "That's the bullet that had my name on it."

Two hours later, after giving her statement and reliving the nightmare, Sonya was exhausted. Brandon had disappeared about an hour ago to offer his services to the investigation even though she knew he wasn't officially on the clock.

The officer next to her flicked a glance behind her and she turned to see Brandon approaching. He touched her arm and she shivered. "Are you all finished?"

"Yes, I believe so."

"Why don't we go over to my office so you— we—can decompress?"

She nodded, noticing the sparks his touch set off. In spite of the terrifying situation they'd just lived through, she was still aware of everything about him. From the moment she'd walked into Finding the Lost last week, every time she was in his presence, her attraction meter spiked. So far she'd been able to ignore it, telling herself she didn't have the time or energy for a relationship.

Especially not with someone she couldn't read.

Brandon's green eyes hadn't revealed anything to her and she hadn't figured out how to discern his moods or thoughts. That threw her off kilter. Of course, she'd known the man only a week. "Are you finished helping here?"

"For now."

They walked across the park toward the office buildings. Sonya averted her gaze from the blood still staining the jogging path. "How long will they keep the park closed?"

"Until a crime-scene cleanup crew gets here and removes all traces of the tragedy."

She nodded, grateful for his easy manner and unhurried gait. "You hear about these kinds of things on the news almost every day, it seems," she said. "But you never really expect it to happen to you, to find yourself fighting to survive in the midst of something so awful."

She wondered if the shooter was gone. Or if he'd managed to avoid detection so he could linger and watch. She wondered if he was reveling in the chaos he'd created. A shiver slithered up her spine and she offered up a silent prayer that he'd be found and unable to hurt anyone else.

Brandon put an arm around her shoulders and she looked up, startled. He dropped his arm. "Sorry. You looked like you needed a friend."

His gruff voice and averted gaze grabbed her.

She touched his arm and gave him a smile. "I do need a friend. Thank you."

He nodded but kept his distance. Regret filled her and she wished she'd just leaned into him and accepted the comfort he'd been offering. She had a feeling he didn't do that very often.

"How's the job going?" he asked as he opened the glass door for her.

She stepped inside the cool interior of the lobby. "It's going fine." She'd been at Spartanburg Regional for only three weeks.

"And your mother's house?"

"Coming along." Her mother had died a month ago. Sonya had moved to South Carolina to settle her mother's affairs. She took a seat. She understood what he was doing. Talking about nothing to get her mind off the shooting. She wished it would work. "Did you find anything about the birth certificate?"

In the process of cleaning out her mother's house, she'd come across a box of baby items. Including a birth certificate for a Heather Bradley.

He nodded. "I did. Interesting enough, Heather Bradley, daughter to Don and Ann Bradley, was kidnapped from a church nursery twenty-eight years ago."

Sonya processed that bit of information and swallowed hard. "Why would my mother have the birth certificate of a kidnapped baby?"

Brandon leaned forward and narrowed his eyes. "That's a very good question. What do you think?"

She reached up and rubbed her forehead, trying to hold the headache at bay. "I don't know. Maybe she found it. She was a yard-sale junkie and something of a hoarder. What if she bought the box, stashed it and never thought about it again?" It had been known to happen. Hadn't it?

"It's possible." He looked doubtful.

"Are you saying you think my parents kidnapped a child?" she scoffed. She pictured her gentle father. A pastor with compassionate eyes and warm bear hugs. Before cancer had stolen his physical body. Cancer had robbed her of both of her parents. A lump formed in her throat. The illness may have taken his body, but his spirit had stayed strong to the end. "No way."

"I'm not saying that at all, but it does raise questions for sure." He paused. "Did anyone live in the house before your family?"

"Yes. The house was a parsonage. My father was a pastor for the church next door. When the church hit some hard times financially, my father decided to buy the house to help them out."

Brandon frowned. "How could he afford to do that if the church was having a tough time?"

Sonya blinked. "I don't know. I never really thought about it. I was only a child. Maybe ten or eleven when it happened."

Brandon tapped his chin and sighed. "Hmm. Well, I'll keep digging."

"Was Heather Bradley ever found?"

"No."

"Oh." Her stomach twisted into a knot.

"But I did locate her family. They actually live about thirty minutes from here, practically across town."

"How was Heather taken? Why would her birth certificate be in her diaper bag? Don't people usually keep those in a safe place?"

He gave her a slow smile that made her heart trip all over itself. His eyes crinkled at the corners. "What?"

"You ask good questions," he said. "I'm impressed. According to Mr. Bradley, his wife had decided to go shopping Saturday afternoon. She checked the mail, and the birth certificate had arrived. She slipped it into the diaper bag so she wouldn't lose it. She said she forgot about it until after Heather was taken."

"Which was the next day. So the kidnapper took the baby and the diaper bag?"

"Right out of the church nursery."

She nodded. "Right. So how did that happen? Where was security? Wouldn't someone see the person taking the child and stop him or her?"

He held up a hand at her rapid-fire questions. "Let me explain. Mrs. Bradley said there were two rooms in the nursery. A room that held cribs for sleeping babies and a monitor. The door was shut so the other children could play without waking the ones sleeping. There was a window in the door, but…" He shrugged. "You have to remember this was almost thirty years ago. Security in church nurseries was nothing like it is today. If they even had security."

"So no one knew Heather was missing until a worker went in the room to check on the other babies."

"Exactly."

"And I found the diaper bag with the birth certificate in my mother's closet." She paused, her mind racing. Then she looked at him and swallowed hard. "Do you think I'm Heather Bradley?"

TWO

Brandon saw the weariness on her face—and a sort of horrified curiosity mixed with embarrassment that she would even consider asking the question. When he didn't answer right away, she pushed him. "Well?"

Brandon shrugged. "I can't say the thought hasn't occurred to me. I think it's a real possibility. We'd have to prove it—or disprove it—of course."

"Of course," she murmured then gave a disbelieving laugh. "I really don't think I could possibly be her. I mean, it just doesn't make sense. I'm not adopted." She swallowed hard. "At least I was never told that I am."

"I understand that you'd feel that way, but I think it's something we need to consider and look into."

She bit her lip and gave a slow nod. "So where do we start?"

"Let me think about it." He rubbed a hand down his face. "You need some rest. Is there anyone that could stay with you tonight?"

She shrugged. "I'll be all right."

"I really don't think you should be alone. Today was traumatic, a tragedy that's already playing on every news channel in the country. You probably have the media camped out on your doorstep."

Sonya froze. "I hadn't thought of that."

He knew she hadn't. "So. Is there anyone you could stay with?"

"I could call Missy Carlisle, I guess."

"Who's that?"

"A friend from work. Even though I haven't been there very long, we've become pretty close."

"Close enough to spend the night?"

"Of course."

He nodded to the device still strapped to her arm. "Is that your phone?"

Sonya looked at her biceps as though she'd never seen it before. "Yes." She released the device from the strap and dialed her friend's number. While she talked, Brandon watched her. When she'd first come into the office, he'd seen her with Erica and wondered about her.

Erica had caught him watching. Later she'd patted his arm and said, "Don't worry, she's the real deal. She's not here to gawk at our resident hero."

Brandon had rolled his eyes. "Cute, sis. I'm not the one who worries about that and you know it."

"Well, you have to admit, thanks to the media,

we've had a few loonies looking to become your next girlfriend."

He couldn't help the wry twist his lips took.

A hero.

Just the thought made him shake his head. He wasn't a hero; he'd just done his job. But the media had dubbed him a hero for being a part of bringing Molly home. Erica's three-year-old daughter had disappeared while on a field trip with her pre-school class.

Brandon had been a detective with the police force in Spartanburg. Banned from working the case because of his relation to Molly, he'd resigned and come on staff full-time with Finding the Lost. They'd brought Molly home three years later. Longer than he'd intended, but at least she was finally home with her mother.

And then he'd been in the right place at the right time two months ago. He'd caught and subdued an abusive husband trying to kidnap his child in the grocery-store parking lot. The media had gone nuts. Grudgingly, he admitted Erica had a point. Put the word *hero* on a guy and things got interesting—and extremely embarrassing. Not too long after the story broke he'd started getting marriage proposals via mail, email and even text messages.

Women. He'd never understand them. And frankly wasn't sure he ever wanted to after the fiasco with his fiancée leaving him. All he'd learned was that most women weren't to be trusted. The only exceptions he knew of were Katie Randall and Erica. He had no doubt they were a different type of woman.

But there was something about Sonya that made him wonder if she fell into the same category as his sister and friend. He also wondered if she ever smiled. A genuine smile, not strained or sad or worried.

She hung up and looked at him. "Missy said that would be fine. I need to go home and get some things, though."

"I'll take you."

Sonya stood. "It's not necessary."

"Maybe not, but I want to."

She tilted her head, and her ragged ponytail flopped onto her left shoulder. She studied him for so long, he almost started to squirm. "Okay."

Her quiet acquiescence stirred his heart. And his mind. Was her innocent little-ole-me an act? Or was Erica right and she was the real deal? He decided he'd have to keep his distance until he figured it out.

Sonya sat in Missy's living area and debated whether or not they were close enough friends for her to share her heart. She noted the Bible on the end table and the plaque on the wall that stated, *As for me and my house, we will serve the Lord.*

Neither one of those necessarily meant Missy practiced what she displayed, but chances were she wouldn't have the items if she didn't.

"What is it?" Missy handed Sonya a mug of steaming coffee flavored with vanilla.

Sonya blew on it, then took a sip. She smiled. "My mother always said one little puff isn't going to make one bit of difference in the temperature."

Missy laughed. "Well, she's right."

"I know but I do it anyway."

Missy sat in the recliner and curled her legs beneath her. "Are you sure you're all right?"

The television played in the background on mute. Fox News carried the latest about the shooting, and Sonya shook her head. "I'm all right. Still shaken up, of course. The whole thing is surreal and I'll probably have nightmares for weeks, but I'm just grateful to be alive." She took another sip of the steaming brew. "How is the woman who was brought in?"

"Still alive when I left an hour ago, but critical."

Sonya leaned her head against the back of the couch. "I don't understand people who can do that kind of thing," she whispered.

"I don't, either, and I don't want to." Missy paused. "So who was the good-looking guy who followed you here?"

Sonya felt the flush creep up into her cheeks. "That's Brandon."

"And? You haven't talked about him at work."

That wasn't her style, but she didn't say that. "I hired him to look into something I found going through my mother's things after she died."

"What'd you find?" Missy turned serious, her brow creasing.

So Sonya spilled her story. Missy stared wide-eyed, her flavored coffee forgotten. Sonya finished with "The shooting happened just across from Brandon's office with Finding the Lost. He heard the shots and came running."

"That's just crazy. And this Heather Bradley was kidnapped twenty-eight years ago?"

"Yes."

"And Brandon works for this company."

"Yes."

"Tell me more about Brandon. You blushed when I asked you about him."

Sonya groaned and gave a half laugh. "I can't figure Brandon out. On the one hand, he's kind, concerned and obviously very good at his job. On the other, he comes across aloof and—suspicious." She'd been aware of his intense scrutiny while she'd been on the phone with Missy, but had pretended not to notice. He'd walked her back to the park and waited while she'd retrieved her car. Very serious, very businesslike. "I don't know." And she didn't. Which meant it was time to change the subject. "I think I'll grab some sleep. What time is your shift tomorrow?"

"Seven A to Seven P." Meaning seven in the morning to seven at night. "What about you?"

"The same, but I'll have to go home and change before I go in."

"I have some clothes and scrubs you can use if you want to borrow them."

She almost took her friend up on the offer. Instead, she said, "I'll just go home early in the morning and get ready. My house is on the way to the hospital, so it's no big deal. And besides, I have to feed Chaucer."

Chaucer, her cat, independent and aloof until it was time to eat, but she'd filled his bowls before her run earlier and he would be physically fine for the next few hours. His temperament would leave a lot to be desired, but she'd deal with that later.

Missy shrugged and yawned. "Okay. Well, if you need anything, feel free to ask or browse."

Sonya smiled. "Thanks. Shampoo and conditioner are all I need for now."

"All right. See you in the morning."

Sonya sat on the couch for a few minutes after Missy padded down the hallway to her bedroom. She stared at the clock on the mantel and listened to it tick.

Each click of the second hand felt like fingernails on a chalkboard.

Now that she was alone, the thought that she could have died today ate at her. "I don't know why You left me here, Lord, but I thank You for that," she whispered. She knew she'd die one day, and she was ready for when it happened. Meaning she knew she'd go to heaven, but until that time, she wanted her life to count, to mean something.

She saw death on a daily basis, but coming face-to-face with the fact that a bullet could have so easily taken her out made her shudder.

And made her all the more determined to find out what had happened to little Heather Bradley. To find out if Brandon's hunch was right and she *was* Heather. Because if she was, her entire life had been a lie.

From his deck, Brandon sat in the darkness, ignoring the humidity that caused sweat to bead across his forehead. He stared at the half-moon and allowed his mind to process the day. At two in the morning, he sipped a soda, a rare drink for him, but one he enjoyed on occasion.

Living in the middle of downtown had its advantages, one of which was proximity to both of his offices. When Jordan Gray had looked him up after his last tour in Iraq, at loose ends and grieving the death of his brother, who'd recently died of an overdose, Brandon had offered him the spare bedroom.

And now Jordan was getting married to Katie Randall this summer. A June wedding Katie admitted she'd dreamed of since she was a little girl, but never really thought would happen. They'd bought a small house about fifteen minutes away and Katie was moving in tomorrow.

After the wedding, Jordan would join her, and Brandon would be left alone. He could afford the payment, but had to admit he'd be a little lonely. Not that things would be much different than they were now. Jordan spent every spare minute with Katie, coming home only to sleep and shower.

First Erica and Max had tied the knot, now Jordan and Katie. Brandon wondered if he'd ever meet someone. Someone real, someone who didn't want to be with him just because the media had labeled him a hero.

His jaw tightened. Then relaxed as Sonya came to mind. She seemed so likable and genuine. He hoped that was the case, but would keep his guard up. His ex-fiancée had seemed quite likable and genuine—until she'd met someone who didn't come with as much baggage attached to him.

Brandon knew he had issues that stemmed from his family situation—and he was working on them. It had hurt when Krystal had decided she didn't want to work on them with him.

Brandon turned to head back inside. The lamp in

his den went out. He stopped. Looked at his kitchen window. The light over the sink was off, too.

For a moment, he stood silent, letting his eyes adjust to the darkness. The town house to his left had power. So did the one to his right.

A blown fuse?

Maybe. But in his line of work, he wasn't going with that assumption.

Brandon set his drink on the small table next to the chair and reached for his weapon. The one that wasn't there because he'd left it on his kitchen counter. Next to his cell phone.

Wary, Brandon slipped to the edge of the deck and waited. Watching through the French doors. Even though it was dark inside, the moon offered a bit of light, coming through the open blinds and into the den.

His patience paid off when a thin shadow moved into his line of sight. The person paused, then moved to his desk. A thin beam of light came from a small penlight. Who was it?

Itching to confront the intruder, Brandon held still, waiting and watching. A weapon appeared for a brief moment, and the large barrel on the end said this was no random break-in.

His gut twisted as he mentally moved into battle mode. His right hand twitched, wanting the comforting feel of his Glock against his palm.

The town house had two levels. Right now, they

were on the bottom level. Upstairs he had three bedrooms. One for him, one for Jordan and one he used as an office. The antique desk in the living area simply served as decoration.

But his intruder didn't know that.

Did the person not realize he was home?

The weapon said yes. The leisurely search of the desk said no. Or he wasn't worried about it.

Brandon waited for a lull in the traffic, then slid the glass door open and slipped inside. He closed the door with a quiet hiss.

The figure at the other end of the town house paused. Lifted his head as though listening. Brandon stayed still, his only thought to get to his weapon. The person moved toward him, his weapon held expertly in front of him.

Brandon took note. Weapons training. Breaking-and-entering training. What else? Not wanting to be caught unprepared and while the element of surprise was still on his side, he moved on silent feet through the darkness to the kitchen.

The intruder's gun popped, flashed. The bullet slammed into the wall next to Brandon's head.

So much for being quiet.

He dived for the kitchen and rolled as another bullet burned a hole in his newly laid tile floor. Anger fizzled. His back hit the cabinets. He lifted his hand and snagged his Glock from the counter, keeping his head low.

He'd been shot before. He had no intention of letting it happen again. With his other hand, he reached up and grabbed his phone.

"Come around the corner and you get shot. Tell me what you want and you might keep breathing." He kept his voice steady. Controlled. He didn't want to shoot anyone. Not even this person intent on killing him. He did, however, want to know who it was. But he wasn't going hunting blind.

Brandon listened as he punched in 911 and pressed the phone to his ear.

Silence from the den. The 911 operator's voice on the other end of the phone sounded incredibly loud. He lowered the phone.

A whisper of movement from the living area reached him. Brandon stilled. Moving closer or moving away?

Brandon tried again. "Get out while the getting's good." He pressed the phone back to his ear and whispered his address.

"Yes, sir. I got it. What's the emergency?"

He didn't answer, just listened.

Still the intruder said nothing and made almost no sound. Brandon waited, nerves bunched, muscles quivering with his tension. A low voice finally came to him. "Stop looking for Heather Bradley."

And then the quiet snick of the door shutting.

Brandon stayed still, ignoring the adrenaline

rush racing at fever pitch through his veins. Was it a trick to get him to show himself? He moved and peered around the kitchen cabinet, into the den area. No movement, but it was so dark, someone could be hunched down and he'd never see him.

Brandon flattened himself on his belly and kept his weapon in front of him. Army crawling, he moved toward the den, eyes probing the darkness.

He could see nothing. He heard nothing. He turned the volume down on the 911 operator frantically trying to get him to answer.

The sirens in the distance caught his attention and he figured they were headed for him. If the intruder was still in his house, he was going to be trapped.

No one spoke. No more shots came his way.

Brandon's adrenaline ebbed as he finally decided he was alone. He stood, still cautious, watchful. He flicked on the small light above his sink, not wanting to turn on the bright kitchen light after being in the darkness for so long. He needed to let his eyes adjust slowly.

Still keeping himself protected from anything that might come from the den area, he waited to make sure.

Then slowly, methodically, he swept each and every room, weapon ready.

The place was empty.

Only now he knew someone didn't want him looking for Heather Bradley. The question was: Why?

That someone had just made a very bad mistake because now Brandon was more determined than ever to get answers to all of his questions. All of them.

THREE

Somehow Sonya made it through her twelve-hour shift without collapsing. She didn't like working on Sundays, but it was part of the job. She was fortunate she had to take only one Sunday a month.

Now she had one more thing to do before she went home to collapse.

She knocked on the door to room 412.

"Come in."

Sonya stepped into the room and saw the woman in the bed. "Hi, Dineen, my name's Sonya Daniels. I was in the park when you were shot."

"You're the one who saved me," she whispered and held up a hand.

Sonya took it and squeezed. "I'm glad you're going to be all right."

"I am, too." She coughed and winced. Sonya handed her the cup of water by her bed. After Dineen took a small sip, she set it aside.

"Is someone staying with you?"

"My husband. He went downstairs to get something to eat. He'll be back soon."

"Good."

"Did they catch him?"

"No, not yet."

She nodded. "I figured I would have heard something if they had. It's still all over the news."

"They'll catch him."

Her lids drooped. "I'm sorry. I can't seem to stay awake very long."

"It's the pain medicine. I just wanted to check on you. Go to sleep and heal."

"Thank you."

Sonya smiled and left. Exhaustion swept over her. All she wanted was to go home and crawl into bed. Even the thought of her empty refrigerator couldn't tempt her into stopping at the grocery store. She would make do with peanut butter and crackers and a bottle of water. Sleep was all she craved.

"Hey, Sonya," Missy called.

Sonya turned. "Yes?"

"Are you going home? Do you need to stay another night at my house?"

"I think I'm all right." She'd managed to dodge the reporters this morning. Security had kept them from her while at work. She wondered if they'd be waiting for her at her car. The thought made her grimace.

"Well, you're welcome to stay if you need to. Just let me know."

"Thanks." Sonya gave her a small smile. It was all she could muster. However, she decided Missy was the real deal and hoped they could build their friendship. She missed having a close friend.

"I'll see she gets home all right."

Sonya turned at the deep voice and found Brandon standing in the small foyer. He looked as tired as she felt. "What are you doing here?"

"I'm fine, thanks. How are you?"

Sonya felt the heat in her neck start to rise and cleared her throat. "I'm sorry. How are you?"

"I'm just teasing. I thought I'd stop by and see if you could use a bite to eat?"

Sonya was amazed to feel energy start to seep back into her tired body. His mere presence jump-started her pulse and made her heart pound. She swallowed hard. "I could eat."

"Great. I want to talk to you about something."

"Like what?"

"Don't mind me. I was just leaving," Missy said.

Sonya felt her flush deepen and she shot Missy a look that said to stop. Missy grinned, waved and headed out the door.

Sonya rolled her eyes and turned back to Brandon, who smiled, his eyes dark and mysterious. She wished she could read him.

"Come on. I'll drive and bring you back when we're done."

She hesitated. "Do you mind if I just follow you?"

He shrugged. "Sure."

He walked her the rest of the way to her car. She slid into the driver's seat and clicked on her seat belt.

Twenty minutes later, she found herself sitting opposite Brandon at one of her favorite cafés about a mile from her mother's home.

Brandon rubbed his coffee cup between his palms. Sonya took a bite of her chicken panini. With food in her stomach, the strong black coffee racing through her veins and the handsome man across from her, she felt as though she'd just had eight hours of sleep. Her watch said it was pushing eight o'clock. If she was in bed by eleven, she would be good to go for tomorrow's shift. "What did you want to talk about?"

"Heather Bradley."

"What about her? Did you find out if—" She bit her lip, unable to voice the question.

"If you're her?"

"Yes. I can't even believe I'm asking. It's just too bizarre."

"Unfortunately, bizarre stuff happens all the time." He smiled. "I've talked to Mr. Bradley once.

He's open to meeting you. Would you be interested in taking the baby stuff to them?"

Sonya paused midbite. "Me?"

"Well, it was in your mother's house where you found the stuff. Mr. Bradley said they'd love to have the bag and other items back."

"But…but…" she sputtered. "Won't they think my parents had something to do with their daughter's kidnapping?"

"He asked what I thought about your parents and how they might have come by the items."

"What did you say?"

"Just that you had come to me with this story and the items and were as confused about them as everyone else."

Sonya took another bite, chewed and swallowed. The distraction gave her time to think. "I'm okay with returning the stuff, then."

"Good. He wants to talk to you. Said he had questions for you."

Sonya shrugged. "I feel sorry he's lost his daughter, but unfortunately, I won't have any answers to his questions."

"I told him that. He wants to see you anyway."

She paused. "Did you tell him we were pondering whether I might be Heather?"

"No. But I think the thought crossed his mind when I told him about you."

"I see." She thought for a few more minutes then nodded. "Well, then. When do we go?"

"As soon as you get off your shift tomorrow night? Or will you be too tired?"

"I'll be tired, but I still want to go. The sooner we get this resolved, the better I'll feel. And I'll ask if I can leave a couple of hours early if that would help."

"It would. So around 5:00?"

"Okay. I don't think it'll be a problem."

"Yo. Brandon, my man, what up?"

Sonya jerked at the voice to her left. She turned to find a tattooed young man with more earrings in his ears than she had in her jewelry box.

Brandon stood and held a hand out to the kid. "Spike. Haven't seen you in a while. How are you?"

"Hanging, dude. Just hanging."

"Staying out of trouble?"

"Of course."

Sonya almost had to laugh at his attempt at an innocent look.

Brandon rolled his eyes, but the smile on his lips was genuine. He turned to her. "Sonya, I'd like you to meet Landon Olsen, aka Spike. Landon, this is Sonya."

"Pretty lady, dude." He elbowed Brandon and winked. Sonya could feel the flush inching its way up her neck and into her cheeks. Brandon gave a gentle slap to Spike's head. The boy laughed and said, "Sorry. I'm kidding you." He made a formal bow in Sonya's direction. "Pleasure to meet you, ma'am."

"Well, thank you, Spike. It's nice to meet you, too." She shot a glance back and forth between the two. "So how do you guys know each other?"

Spike stuck out his well-muscled chest. "I'm one of his more successful projects."

Sonya lifted a brow at Brandon and he groaned. "He's a pain in my side most of the time."

Spike grinned. "Dude, you know you're my hero." He looked at Sonya. "I'm gonna be a detective like him one day."

"That's a wonderful goal, Spike," she said. "I have a feeling you'll be one of the best and brightest."

Spike's eyes lit up and she could see he took her compliment seriously. Just the way she meant it. He turned to Brandon. "I like her, man. Don't mess it up." Before Brandon could say anything, Spike announced, "Hey, I gotta go, dude. See you Saturday?"

"I'll be there."

"I'm going to beat you so bad, you're going to need a doctor to put you back together."

"Don't count on it. Your head's getting so big, it's going to weigh you down."

Spike barked his laughter, gave a two-fingered salute and slipped out the door.

Sonya sat back. "What in the world? Beat you?"

Brandon blew out a sigh. "I help out at Parker House. It's a place that takes in young men who've had some brushes with the law and rehabilitates them. Or at least tries to. It's part that and part recreation center. When he said he was going to beat me, he meant he was going to win our game of three-on-three this weekend."

"Basketball?"

"Yes."

"Sounds like fun."

He studied her. "You like basketball?"

"Love it."

"You want to come watch?"

She did. "What time?"

"Nine o'clock."

She groaned. "As in a.m.? On a Saturday morning?"

He laughed. "Not a morning person?"

"Not in the least. I mean, I have to be for work, of course, but on my days off…"

"You almost smiled."

She frowned. "What?"

"You don't smile much."

"I haven't had much to smile about lately." She tried to force her lips into one and he shook his head.

"I'm not talking about a fake smile. I'm talking about a real one." Before she had a chance to respond or even try to find a "real" smile, he said, "But you'll come?" His voice softened and he leaned forward. She caught a look in his eyes that made her gulp.

"Sure. I'll come."

He nodded and looked away. She wondered what he was thinking, but couldn't tell. Did he regret asking her? He cleared his throat. "Anyway, tomorrow after your shift, we'll go see Heather's parents."

So it was back to business. "Yes. That's fine."

Brandon studied Sonya and wondered what had come over him that he would invite her into a place that he kept as his. His home was his haven. Parker House was his escape, his passion. And he'd just invited Sonya to come. He must be more tired than he thought. "I wanted to talk to you about something else. Someone broke into my house last night."

She gaped at him. "Broke into your house?"

He nodded and told her what had happened.

"But why?" she asked.

"To tell me to stop looking for Heather Bradley."

She paled and sat back. "What?"

He took a sip of his coffee. "I think it's extremely weird that you were shot at yesterday and then someone breaks in my house the same night. It could be just a crazy coincidence, but I've been in this business a long time and I'm just not sure I'm going to buy that theory."

"I don't know, Brandon. The shooter wasn't really going for me personally. He was shooting at others in the park, too."

"True. I've thought about that. And maybe I'm just grasping at straws trying to link the two things."

"What else did the person say?"

He shook his head. "Nothing. Whoever it was didn't get to stay long enough. When he realized I had a weapon, he took off. The cops got there and we searched the area, but came up empty."

He saw her swallow. "I'm so sorry."

"I am, too."

"Do you have any enemies?"

"I think a better question is, do we have any enemies in common?"

"But we've only known each other a couple of weeks."

Brandon lifted a brow. Had it been such a short time? It seemed as if he'd known her a lot longer. "Exactly. The only thing we have in common is your case."

"Heather Bradley."

"Yes."

"So someone doesn't want us looking for her? But who would even know?"

He shrugged. "I honestly don't know, but it's the only reasonable explanation I can come up with. But most likely you're right. The two incidents probably aren't connected."

"You don't have an alarm system?"

"I don't."

"I'm surprised."

He gave a low chuckle. "I never really felt the need for it. I don't have anything worth stealing and I have a gun on my nightstand and know how to use it." He paused. "After last night I might reconsider, though."

"So what now?"

"Now we watch our backs."

"But we keep looking for Heather?"

"Absolutely."

She nodded, relief in her eyes. "Good. I really want to know who she is—or was." Her jaw firmed. "And prove it's not me."

It hit Brandon that Sonya didn't have a deceptive bone in her body. The realization allowed him to relax a fraction. She wasn't after him because of some silly hero status that had been dumped on him. And she wasn't interested in him romantically.

The sharp pang of regret surprised him. Made

him look at her a little closer. And he decided that if she wasn't a client, he'd be asking her out.

He drew in a deep breath at the silent admission.

"Are you okay? You have a funny look on your face."

Brandon cleared his expression. "I'm fine. Are you ready to go?"

Her brows knit but she nodded. "Sure."

Together they walked out of the restaurant and he escorted her to her car, his nerves alert, senses sharp. At her car, she started to slide in the driver's seat when he noticed a small square of paper about the size of an index card under her windshield wiper. "What's this?"

He handed it to her and leaned in to read along with her. "'Stop looking for Heather Bradley. She doesn't want to be found.'"

FOUR

Sonya gaped. "Well, I guess we're making some-one kind of nervous."

"You think?" A muscle jumped in his jaw as he stared at the note.

"So what do we do?"

Brandon lifted a brow. "Do you want to stop looking for her?"

"No way."

"Do you have a paper bag in your car?"

"No, I don't think so."

"All right, let's go back in the restaurant and get one."

Sonya shut her belongings in the car and followed Brandon, who carried the note between his thumb and forefinger. She figured he wanted to get the note tested for fingerprints. She glanced around the parking lot, wondering if the person who'd left the note was watching. Shivers slid up and down her spine.

Spooked, she stayed close to the person who

seemed to represent the only security she could find in a world that had shifted on its axis once again. First the death of her father, then her mother and now someone was sending her threats.

She didn't like it.

Sonya waited by the door while Brandon requested a paper bag. The waitress handed him one and he slipped the note inside and folded the bag over. He held it up. "All right, I'm going to take this over to the lab."

"Tonight?"

He shrugged. "Why not?"

"But it's late. You've had a full day and need to rest." She sighed. "And I sound like your mother. I'm going to be quiet now, get in my car and go home."

His lips pulled into a smile. A smile he seemed to struggle with. Almost as though he didn't do it very often and his lips had forgotten how. She knew exactly how he felt. Smiling seemed to take more effort than it was worth these days.

"I'll follow you home before I take this over," he said. "I have a friend who works the graveyard shift. He'll probably be able to take care of this pretty quick. Depends on what else he has in the lineup."

"Okay. Thanks." She walked to the door and stepped outside. Her eyes immediately scanned the area for any threat. "And I think after today's craziness, I would appreciate you following me home." She paused. "And going through my house to make sure no one is inside would be nice, too."

"My pleasure."

His hand slipped under her elbow, and warmth danced up her arm. What was it about this man at her side? It was rather crazy the feelings he'd stirred up in her. And the feelings had her curious, too. She'd felt attraction before. Had even dated a doctor at the hospital before she'd moved to South Carolina to be with her mother during those hard final days of her life. So why now? Why would her heart suddenly decide that it was time to be attracted to Brandon, a man so tightly closed emotionally, a crowbar wouldn't get him to open up?

A hand waved in front of her face. "Where are you?"

Sonya blinked and found herself at her car. "I was lost in thought."

"I could see that. About what?"

She shrugged. "Everything. How confusing my life has suddenly become."

"We'll get to the bottom of this," Brandon said. "I promise."

She smiled. "I know you'll try."

"Well, that smile's not fake, but it looks a little sad." He held the door for her while she slipped into the driver's seat.

"Thanks."

He closed her door and she waited for him to get into his car. He flashed his lights when he was ready and she pulled from the parking lot.

She kept an eye on her rearview mirror and couldn't help wondering while Brandon was following her, was someone following him?

Brandon was concerned. The shooting in the park could have been a random thing. As unfortunate as it was, that kind of thing happened and made the news all the time. Okay, maybe not all the time, but often enough that people were no longer shocked when they saw reports on the news. Saddened, angry and frightened that their world could be such a dangerous place, but not shocked.

But the break-in at his house and the note left on Sonya's car both pointed to the fact that someone didn't want them looking for Heather Bradley. That was one fact he had no trouble figuring out.

By the time they pulled into Sonya's driveway, he'd mapped out his plan of action for the next day.

She pulled into her garage and he met her as she climbed out of her car. "Nice place."

"Thanks. My mother was originally from South Carolina before she and my father met. Then she went to college in Virginia and my dad swept her off her feet." She gave a small smile and led him into the house via the back door. "At least that's her version."

"Your father had a different one?" He stepped into her kitchen. Cinnamon and another spicy scent hit him and he drew in a deep breath.

"Absolutely. He said Mom swept *him* away." The fondness in her voice got to him.

He stopped at the table and looked into her eyes. Which made him crave chocolate.

At the same time, a long-rooted bitterness he'd thought he'd managed to suppress rose up strong and hot, taking him by surprise. "My parents never felt that way about each other."

Something in his tone must have caught her attention. Her gaze sharpened. "I'm sorry."

"So am I." Now he wanted the subject dropped. Him and his big mouth. "I don't know why I told you that. Forget it." He moved away from her. "Stay here while I check out the house."

He could tell his abrupt departure confused her but he had to get away. He felt his walls slipping, crumbling before her sweet disposition and compassionate eyes. *She's a client, Hayes, remember that. You don't date clients.*

With his weapon ready, he checked the den, the three bedrooms and three bathrooms. He opened doors and peered in every potential hiding place, taking note that she kept a clean house. The glass on the nightstand, the T-shirt over the footboard of the bed and the flip-flops tossed into the corner of the room said she wasn't obsessive about everything being in its place, though. "It's clear, Sonya," he said. He returned to the kitchen to find her staring out the window over the sink. "Sonya?"

She jerked and spun, a pretty cat in her arms. She stroked the animal's head and blinked. "Oh. Sorry. I was lost in thought. Again."

"It's okay. I just said your house is clear."

She let out a relieved breath and set the cat on the floor. "Thank you. Once I lock the door behind you I'll feel all right."

"Who's your friend?"

"That's Chaucer. He's a pretty independent little guy, but when I'm gone for a long time, he likes to be held for a few minutes when I first walk in." The cat sniffed Brandon's shoes and must have decided he was okay as he rubbed against Brandon's leg.

Brandon leaned over and scratched the cat's ears while he debated whether Sonya should feel safe behind her locked doors or not. How serious was the person who'd left the note on her car? Pretty serious if it was the person who'd broken into his house to deliver the same message.

She must have sensed his hesitation. She walked over and patted his arm. "I'll be fine."

Brandon still paused, wondering if he should leave. Finally, he said, "All right. I'll see you tomorrow?"

"At five."

"At five." Brandon forced himself to walk away and climb into his car. He gave the area one last sweep and didn't see anything that made his nerves spike into alert mode.

But that didn't mean it wasn't there.

Sonya twisted the dead bolt. The lock clicked and silence descended. She shuddered as the house took on an ominous feel now that she was all alone. "Stop it," she muttered.

Exhaustion swamped her. She had to get some sleep. Seven in the morning would come fast.

And yet, how could she sleep knowing someone felt threatened enough to leave a note on her car? And to break into Brandon's house…

All of a sudden, she didn't feel so safe. Her locks looked flimsy and she couldn't remember if her bedroom window was latched.

Swallowing hard against the fear that wanted to take hold of her, she headed to her bedroom. At the entrance, she paused. "He said it was clear. There's no one in there."

Saying the words out loud helped, but still…

She stepped over the threshold and went straight to the window, felt the latch and found it locked. Her breath whooshed from her lungs. "Get a grip, girl."

After a quick shower, she threw on a T-shirt and cotton shorts and turned the air conditioner down a notch. She kept her cell phone close. A glance at the clock made her grimace. Almost ten o'clock. The thought of falling asleep and having someone break in while she lay unaware made her stomach turn.

For the next thirty minutes, she paced and prayed. And listened. Nothing happened. No one tried to get in.

She sank onto the couch, pulled a blanket around her and rubbed her bleary eyes. She leaned her head back and sighed. Chaucer hopped up in her lap and nuzzled her chin. She rubbed his ears and he purred.

A noise from the kitchen.

She jerked, breath hitching. Chaucer jumped to the floor with a protesting meow.

Then Sonya realized it was only the ice maker. She got up to pace again, angry with herself and the fear she couldn't seem to kick. She had to sleep if she was going to be worth anything tomorrow at work.

Sonya sidled up to the window and looked out. Then blinked in surprise. A strange car sat snugged up next to her curb. She drew back, fear flushing through her once more. Was there someone in the car? Another peek through the window confirmed someone in the driver's seat. Okay, someone in the car was watching her house. Why? Who?

Had the other incidents not happened, she wouldn't have jumped to that conclusion, but at this point and after everything she'd been through, she was going to go with that first thought. Someone was watching her.

Sonya pulled her phone from her pocket and hit the number to speed-dial Brandon. She hated to wake him, but needed him to know about the car.

"Hello?"

"Hi, this is Sonya."

"What's up? Are you okay?"

"I'm sorry to call you so late, but I wanted you to know there's a car parked out in front of my house on the curb and there's someone in the driver's seat."

"Ah. That's Frankie Lee. He's a buddy of mine. He's a detective and also helps out at Parker House. I didn't feel right leaving you all alone and called him to be your backup."

Relief and a smidgen of anger swept through her. "That would have been nice to know."

A slight pause. She thought she might have hurt his feelings. "Sorry. I thought you might have gone on to sleep and I didn't want to wake you," he said, the stiffness in his voice making her wince.

The anger faded as fast as it had surfaced. "No, it's fine. Wonderful, in fact. I'm sorry I snapped. The truth is, I was having trouble settling down.

Now that I know someone is watching out for me, I'll be able to sleep."

"Well, good." The stiffness was gone. "I'm dropping this letter off at the lab, then I'm heading home for a couple of hours of sleep. I'll see you after your shift."

"Sounds good." She paused.

"You need something else?"

"No, no. I guess I just wanted to say thank you."

"You're welcome, Sonya." His low voice turned husky and warm, and shivers danced up her spine with the three words. And the way he said her name. She liked it. It made her feel—cared for. Something she hadn't felt since her mother died.

She hung up and with one last relieved glance out the window headed for her room to get some much-needed sleep. And while glad for the security outside her home, she couldn't help the niggling of unease that inched up her spine. Somehow she knew that while she might sleep easier tonight, the person watching her wasn't far away.

He was waiting—and planning—for the next moment to strike.

FIVE

Monday morning Brandon glanced at the clock on his desk at the police station and rubbed his chin. He'd snagged only a few hours of sleep last night, yet they'd been enough to refresh him.

Knowing Sonya was at work and under the watchful eye of Frankie, Brandon had felt comfortable enough to come in and work on his cases without worrying himself to death about her safety.

Brandon knew Frankie would call him if something came up. He hoped nothing did, of course. And now, in an hour, he'd pick up Sonya at the hospital and take her to meet Heather Bradley's family. Time had slowed to a crawl and he had to force himself to focus. However, excitement stirred inside him, distracting him.

He wasn't sure if it was the thought of seeing Sonya again or the possibility of discovering she was a missing child from twenty-eight years ago.

He stopped to consider that. Wariness rose as he realized seeing Sonya rated higher on his excitement meter than finding out if she was a Bradley. He'd have to add another layer to the crumbling wall around his heart.

His phone rang as he kept up the internal dialogue about why he couldn't allow a romantic interest in Sonya to grow. "Yeah?"

"Tough day?"

Holt Granger, his buddy at the lab. Finally. "Not especially. Why?"

"You sound grumpy."

"I'm not grumpy."

"You sure? Because you sound grumpy."

Brandon sighed. "I'm sure."

"Whatever."

"And no, my day has not been especially hard. I was just thinking about something."

"Something that put you in a bad mood obviously."

Brandon felt his lips twitch. Holt never had a bad day. Or if he did, he didn't let on. "Do you have something that's going to improve my mood?"

"Thought you weren't in a bad mood."

"I said I wasn't grumpy. I didn't say anything about my mood."

Holt laughed and Brandon's small smile curved higher. "Well?"

"I got a print off the letter."

"You're right. My mood just got better. Any matches?"

"No, sorry. Whoever the print belongs to isn't in the system."

"You just tanked my mood."

Holt chuckled then turned serious again. "Nothing from your condo, either. Your intruder had on gloves."

"Yeah. I know."

"I'll stay in touch and let you know if anything else comes up."

"Thanks."

Brandon hung up and looked at the clock again, realized what he was doing and rolled his eyes. His uncharacteristic impatience had him cranky and irritable in spite of his denials to Holt.

But he finally admitted his impatience stemmed from his desire to see Sonya again. He grabbed his keys and his phone and headed out the door. He'd be early, but at least he'd be moving instead of staring like a lovesick schoolboy at the clock on his desk.

At 4:55 in the afternoon, Sonya waved to Frankie Lee, her subtle bodyguard who leaned against the wall and pretended to read a magazine. He returned her wave with a nod and she gathered her things. He sauntered over and pushed the door to the locker room open. "Anyone in here?"

"Just me." Gerri Aimes exited the locker room and gave Frankie the once-over. He seemed to meet her approval because she winked at Sonya. "It's all yours."

"Thanks." Sonya didn't bother to correct her coworker's misunderstanding about who Frankie was. Instead, she stepped into the empty room where she'd change into her street clothes and freshen up a bit before heading down to meet Brandon. Just the thought made her smile. In spite of Brandon's observation that she didn't smile much. She'd noticed lately that when she thought of him, her lips automatically curved upward. She had to admit, too, that while on the job, she occasionally used the smile Brandon called fake. Even that was better than a frown. Or an expressionless facade.

Hospice could be such a heavy place. No one who came to hospice left alive, and families were grieving—some openly, some hiding it well. Others were angry that the medical staff couldn't miraculously heal the dying loved one.

Sonya didn't take it personally, but dealing with them didn't make it any less emotionally draining. And while smiling usually came naturally to her, lately, it had been hard to find something to smile about. She was glad to let her lips relax in the privacy of the locker room.

Not everyone could do her job. She knew that and took comfort in the fact that she was needed even if being needed did come with a high emotional price tag. But she loved what she did and the families she worked with. So she coped with prayer and offered comforting embraces and empathetic tears.

Watching her parents die had given Sonya the desire to reach out to others, to let them know she knew exactly what they were going through. And offer genuine smiles when she could find them.

Some days she saw the results of her efforts. Other days she just prayed she'd made a difference.

Today was one of those days, so she prayed while she changed.

She would see Brandon in five minutes. Give or take a minute or two. She'd gotten permission to leave early, stating she had a personal issue to take care of.

Her nerves hummed and her brain whirled. Who were the Bradleys? What if she was Heather? Her throat tightened at the thought. No way. There just *had* to be a reasonable explanation for everything. Didn't there?

She finished changing and closed the locker door. Another locker door shut with a click.

Footsteps to her left.

The lights went out.

In the dark, Sonya froze and listened. The inky blackness pressed in on her. "Hello?" She thought she was the sole occupant of the locker room since she was the only one leaving two hours before the shift ended.

Had the entire hospital lost power? But why hadn't the generator kicked in?

She moved with shuffling steps toward the door, not wanting to bang her knees on the benches.

Another footfall landed somewhere in front of her, between her and the door. She stopped, her heart picking up speed. "Who's there?"

When she didn't get an answer, but knew someone was definitely in the room with her, her heart kicked it up another notch. With all of the strange things that had happened lately, she wasn't taking any stupid chances.

Sonya shut her mouth and moved sideways. She hit a bench and set her bag on it. She wanted to reach in the bag and search for her cell phone, but didn't dare make the noise she'd have to make in order to find the thing.

So, making no sound, she twisted the strap of her purse around her fingers and stepped around the bench, her soft-soled tennis shoes quiet on the tile floor.

With her pulse pounding in her ears, she moved toward the door once again, hoping whoever had been there seconds before had moved. Another muffled scrape reached her. The person still blocked Sonya's exit.

She slipped back and into one of the bathroom stalls. And wondered if that was possibly the dumbest thing she could have done.

* * *

At ten after five, Brandon started to get a little nervous. Where was she? He was parked at the top of the circle next to the front door where she said she'd meet him. Maybe she'd gotten held up. He tried her number and frowned when she didn't answer. He called Frankie. "Where's Sonya?"

"She's changing in the locker room. Taking her a while, though. I was just getting ready to check on her."

"Did you clear it before she went in?"

"I did. Another woman was in there and came out when Sonya went in."

Brandon waffled. "Give her another minute then knock on the door." He should have put a woman on her. Would have made it easier to keep tabs on her in the bathrooms.

"Of course."

Brandon waited for all of fifteen seconds, then got out of his car and headed for the entrance. He was probably overreacting but he'd rather play it safe. He couldn't believe how worried he was. Telling himself he was being silly, that Frankie had it under control, he nevertheless hurried to the elevator.

Sonya held her breath then let it out in a slow, soundless hiss. She'd lost track of how many seconds—minutes?—had passed since she'd stepped into the stall. Two? Three? And yet, she heard nothing. No footsteps, no one breathing. Nothing.

She was beginning to think it really was her imagination after all, but her gut said it wasn't.

She opened the stall door and stepped out.

From behind her, she felt movement. She started to turn and gasped when something hard, cold and sharp touched her throat and pressed. Sharp, stinging pain froze her. "This is your last warning. Stop looking for Heather Bradley." The knife dug a little deeper. Sonya felt a warm trickle of blood begin to slide down her throat. She let out a whimper, lifted up on her tiptoes. She couldn't speak, was afraid to move. One wrong slip of his hand and the blade would end it all.

The knife lowered and she shoved back against her attacker. The figure stumbled. She heard the knife clatter to the tile floor. Sonya spun away and lunged for the door. A hand gripped her collar and yanked her back.

A knock on the door made her attacker pause. Sonya swung around with her fist and connected with a cheekbone. He cried out and cursed, but let go.

"Sonya? Are you in here?"

"Missy! Get back!" Sonya moved and slammed into the bench. Pain shot through her knee and she heard Missy scream as the man raced through the open door. Sonya spun to see Missy shoved against the door and the dark-clothed figure disappear around the corner. Commotion escalated like a cresting wave. She thought she heard Frankie holler, then pounding feet.

Sonya sank to the floor and lifted a hand to her bleeding throat, wondering how deep the wound was. Weakness invaded her. Mentally, she knew she needed to get up and get help, but her body wouldn't cooperate with her. Shock held her in a tight grip.

Then Brandon was beside her. "I need a doctor in here!" To Sonya, he said, "Let me see." He removed her hand and she thought she saw relief flash in his eyes. "I think it's just a surface wound."

"It stings," she whispered, "but doesn't really hurt. My knee hurts worse." She tried to laugh but wasn't sure she succeeded when he grimaced.

"Sonya?"

She glanced up at Dr. Eddie Ryan's concerned voice.

"Hey, Eddie," she whispered. Security and police officers were already on the scene. They must have been close by. The observation almost made her laugh. She'd just had her throat cut and she was thinking about the proximity of law enforcement. Too bad they hadn't been around when she'd been attacked.

Brandon moved back and let Eddie take his spot.

"Who did this?" Eddie asked without taking his eyes from her neck.

She shrugged. "I'm not sure. Someone who's decidedly unhappy with me. Is Missy okay?"

"I'm fine."

Hearing Missy's shaky voice sent relief pouring through her.

"Unhappy with you?" Eddie snorted. "I'll say." He looked up and spoke to one of the nurses. "Let's get her into a vacant room. Looks like she might need a stitch or two. Call the pharmacy and get me a prescription for an antibiotic." He wrote the script, then looked back at Sonya. "I'm assuming your tetanus vaccination is up to date."

"Yes."

"Good."

She looked at Brandon. "Where's Frankie?"

"He went after your attacker," he said. "Security is helping him. We should hear in a bit that he's in custody. Now, let's get you taken care of."

Then hands were helping her into the wheelchair that had been called for. "I don't need this. I can walk."

"Sh." Brandon laid a hand on her shoulder. "Sit."

Since she didn't think she could stand, much less walk as she'd said she could do, she bit her tongue on any further protests.

Thirty minutes later, she had two black stitches

in the worst part of the cut, had downed the pre-scribed antibiotic and was waiting impatiently for Brandon to reappear. Thankfully, the wound was numb and she wasn't in any pain at the moment, but she was grateful for the little bottle of pain pills in her purse for when the numbing medicine wore off.

She wanted to go home and sleep, but more than that, she wanted to head over to the Bradleys' house. Brandon had wanted to cancel the meeting, but she'd asked him to just postpone it if that was all right with the Bradleys. She didn't want to wait a moment longer than necessary to talk to them.

Doubtful, he'd done as she'd asked and now she itched to go. To get the visit over with. To determine once and for all that she was *not* Heather Bradley.

SIX

Brandon's phone rang as he turned onto the Bradleys' street three hours later than their original appointment. When he'd called to tell the Bradleys what had happened to Sonya at the hospital, Don Bradley had expressed his concern, but made it clear that he didn't care how late it was; he and his wife wanted to see Sonya. As long as she felt up to it.

She'd assured him she did.

Brandon grabbed his cell on the third ring. "Hello?"

"Got some information for you." Hector Gonzales, his partner. Brandon had called him shortly after the attack on Sonya and asked him to help with the investigation. His boss, Sergeant Christine Adams, had given them the green light.

"Let me have it."

"We reviewed the hospital security video footage. Basically, it tells us nothing. Everyone who entered looked like they were supposed to be there.

There's no one running away except for when he pushed his way out of the locker room and disappeared in all the chaos."

"Down the stairwell that was right next to the locker room," Brandon muttered.

"Yeah."

"But how did he get in the locker room without anyone noticing?"

"He wore a wig. We found it in the trash on the next floor. Holt has it and will test it for any stray hairs from the attacker's head. I'm hoping for some DNA to match up to any suspects we're able to haul in. I think I've found the guy in the security video. He wore that nondescript brown wig and was dressed in blue scrubs."

"Just like everyone else in the building."

"Exactly."

"And the other cameras?"

"Not much. If I've got the right person, on his way out, the figure was dressed in black with a hood pulled up obscuring his face. If that's not him, we've got nothing. I've checked and double-checked the footage of people leaving the hospital shortly after the attack, and other than that one possibility, there's nothing. I mean, people are leaving work and they carry large bags. He could have stashed a bag somewhere, went to it and stuffed his clothes in there."

"Or he ditched them." Brandon paused as he

thought. "Okay, so the attacker either got rid of the clothes and left looking totally different or…"

"…he didn't leave right away," Hector said.

"But he might have still tossed the clothes."

"I have a team still going through the trash." He sighed. "And I'll have the hospital send out an emergency email to be on the lookout for blue scrubs in a trash bin."

"With orders not to touch, but call us immediately."

"Exactly. I'll be in touch."

"Thanks."

He hung up and found Sonya watching him. He filled her in on the conversation and she nodded. "I didn't expect it to be very easy to catch this person."

"No, not easy. But not impossible. No one is perfect, and as soon as he makes a mistake, we'll get him." He tapped his fingers against the wheel, his brain whirling. "Are you sure it was a man?"

She blinked at him. "Yes, pretty sure. If it was a woman, she had a pretty deep voice." She rubbed her head. "And when he had me held against him, he felt muscular. Like he worked out. His chest was like a brick." She paled and swallowed hard. "I couldn't move, he was so strong."

He could see the memory shook her. Brandon parked in front of the Bradleys' house. He reached over to grasp her fingers in his. "It's okay. You're safe now."

She nodded. "Right. For now." Her eyes flicked to her surroundings. He'd pulled to a stop at the top of the horseshoe-shaped drive. Brick with white columns, the front porch ran the length of the home. White rockers and a swing gave it a comfortable appearance. Homey. The manicured yard glistened from the sprinklers that had shut off as they drove up the drive.

Their wealth didn't take him by surprise. He'd done his homework, but Sonya's openmouthed stare said this wasn't what she'd expected. "They have money."

"A lot of it."

"From what?"

"Ann's family owns a textile business that's employed by the government. Don works for her father. Their company supplies a lot of the thread that makes uniforms for the armed forces."

"Wow."

"Yeah. What's really wow is that they live very much below their means."

The front door opened and a man with sandy-blond hair stepped onto the porch. If he had any gray, Brandon couldn't see it. Don Bradley's wide smile clearly displayed his pleasure that they'd arrived. The sun still hung low in the sky, but in another fifteen minutes it would be dark.

"You ready?"

"I'm ready." He saw her pull in a deep breath, and then she opened the door and stepped out.

Brandon did the same. Deep breath and all.

Mr. Bradley headed for them, hand outstretched. "Brandon Hayes?"

"Yes, sir. Nice to meet you."

The men shook hands and Brandon was impressed with the man's firm grip and eye contact. "Thanks for coming."

"Of course."

And then he turned to Sonya. The two locked eyes and studied each other. Brandon swallowed hard.

Even he could see the resemblance.

Same dark eyes, same blond hair. Or maybe he was just seeing things. Just because they both had blond hair and dark eyes didn't mean she was the man's daughter.

Don Bradley held out his hand to Sonya, who took it. "Hello, Sonya."

"Hello, Mr. Bradley." Her voice shook slightly and Brandon wondered if she was seeing the same thing he was. Possibly.

"It's Don. For now. Come in, come in." He waved them toward the front door. Brandon gripped the brown bag that held the baby items Sonya had given him when she'd first hired him and followed the two of them inside.

The foyer held a grand crystal chandelier that illuminated the area. The staircase to the left led upstairs. Don led them into the living room to the right. "Have a seat. My wife should be here soon. She went to the gym to work out." He shook his head. "World War Three could break out and she'd still be at the gym. She never misses her workout. She texted and said she was about ten minutes away." He eyed the bag in Brandon's hand and swallowed. "Is that it?"

"Yes, sir."

He nodded. "Might be best for me to take a look before she gets here anyway."

Brandon handed him the bag.

The man clutched it and took a deep breath. A fine tremor ran through his fingers. He looked up. "You know, I never gave up hope that she would come home. I figured anyone who would kidnap an infant wouldn't kill her." His Adam's apple bobbed. "So, I've always believed she was still alive, still out there. We finally adopted. We have a son who's twenty-two. He just graduated college last year and is working as an accountant in Texas."

So, if she was Heather, she would acquire a brother. Brandon's eyes met Sonya's. Her lashes fluttered as she blinked back tears.

Then Don's face hardened. "We've had people who claimed to be Heather, you know. People who've actually knocked on our door and said they were our daughter." He cleared his throat. "Can you believe there are people who go looking for unsolved missing-children cases? Children who belonged to wealthy families and were never found? They take that case, research it, learn it and build an entire story about how they are the missing child?" He shook his head. "It's unbelievable. We investigated each and every one, of course, but they were all frauds."

"That's awful. I'm so sorry," Sonya whispered.

He nodded and opened the bag. When he pulled out the brown Gucci baby tote he gasped. His eyes widened and he stared at Sonya. "It's her bag."

Brandon frowned. "I told you it was."

"I know, but I mean, you really have it. I didn't expect—" He spun it around. "And the pen mark is even there," he whispered. "I was writing a check and juggling Heather at the same time. My pen slipped and I hit the bag."

The front door opened and a woman in workout clothes stepped into the foyer. She dropped her gym bag on the floor and slipped off her tennis shoes. Her ponytail swung around her head. Brandon thought she looked amazing for being in her mid-fifties. In fact, she really didn't look a day over forty.

She turned to see them in the living room and gave them a smile. "Hello."

The smile faltered as she caught sight of the bag in her husband's hands. She paled and actually swayed. Brandon moved fast and caught her by the upper arm. She let him lead her to the sofa and help her sit. And still she never took her eyes from the bag. "How?" she whispered. "Where—"

"My mother had it in her closet," Sonya said.

The woman's stunned gaze turned to Sonya. "And you think you're Heather?"

"Actually, no. I don't."

That seemed to take Mrs. Bradley by surprise. Her perfectly arched brow lifted and some of the shock slid from her face. "You don't?" Suspicion clouded her gaze and she scowled. "Well, that's a new approach."

"Ann—" her husband cautioned.

She ignored him. "Do you know that you're not the first person to come to us and claim to be our long-lost daughter?"

Sonya swallowed hard. "I'm sorry. But I'm not claiming to be your daughter. If anything, I'm here to prove I'm not. My parents were wonderful and I had a lovely childhood, but ever since I've started looking for Heather Bradley, I've been attacked and threatened."

"What?" Mrs. Bradley jerked. "What happened? Attacked and threatened by who?"

Brandon filled them in on the incidents. Mrs. Bradley paled even more if that was possible.

"Oh, dear. That's simply awful. And you're sure all of that happened because you're looking for our daughter?"

Sonya shrugged. "The person was pretty specific about how I needed to stop looking for Heather Bradley."

Mrs. Bradley lifted a hand to rub her forehead. "This is giving me a headache." She sighed and brushed away a tear. "Of course, no one wants Heather found more than I do, but I'm afraid you're wasting your time. We've looked for her for years and have come up with nothing. What makes you think you can find her now?"

Sonya stared at the woman and pondered her question before it hit her. "Because someone who knows we're looking for her feels threatened enough to lash out and tell us to stop."

The room fell silent. Mrs. Bradley nodded and ran a hand over her messy ponytail. She picked up the bag she'd dropped upon entering the foyer. "I'm going to take a shower. I can't deal with this right now." Her voice cracked and she cleared her throat. "I've tried to accept that she's gone, and every time someone brings her up, it just opens up that old wound. It's like pouring alcohol over it. And I can't do it anymore. I just can't," she whispered and ran up the stairs.

Sonya winced. "I'm so sorry."

Mr. Bradley shook his head and she caught a

glimpse of his own tears before he blinked hard. "It's all right. I suppose I shouldn't have gotten her hopes up by telling her you were coming. I should have just found out for sure before saying a word." He looked at Sonya. "But you do look a little like me. I wonder if there's a reason for that or if it's just dumb luck."

Brandon clasped his hands in front of him. "There's one way to find out."

Mr. Bradley lifted a brow. "How's that?"

"DNA testing. We can test you and Mrs. Bradley against Sonya or if you have something of Heather's from when she was born. A lock of hair or—"

Mr. Bradley shook his head. "No. I don't have anything."

"Yes, we do." Mrs. Bradley had returned and now stood at the bottom of the steps.

"What?" Don asked.

"A lock of hair taken the day she was born."

"But—" he started to protest, and then his eyes widened and he nodded. "I know what you're talking about. I'll get it."

"No. I'll do it." She jogged up the stairs.

"I can take it over to my buddy at the lab and see what he comes up with," Brandon said to Mr. Bradley. "It may take some time depending on what he's working on now, but it would give us a definite answer as to whether it matches Sonya."

"Fine. We've waited this long. I don't suppose a few more days—or weeks—will matter much." He looked toward the stairs and frowned. "Let me check on her. Whenever she starts going through Heather's baby book, she gets so upset."

"That's understandable," Sonya murmured, sympathy etched on her face.

"I'll be right back." He ascended the stairs and Sonya met Brandon's gaze.

"Maybe this was a bad idea," she murmured.

"No, I don't think so. If you're Heather then you need to be reunited with your family. If you're not Heather, I'd really like to know why someone doesn't want her found." He paused. "I'd actually like to know that regardless."

"I would, too. But did you see Mrs. Bradley's face? This is really painful for her."

He drew in a deep breath, then let it out through his nose. "I saw. And I hate it for her, but—"

"Here we are." Mr. Bradley stepped into the living room and held out a small envelope. He glanced up the steps. "I gave it to them, dear. Go on and take your shower." Sonya heard receding footsteps. "Ann isn't coming back down. It's simply too much for her."

Brandon took it, held it gently. "I'm sorry this is bringing your pain back." He tapped the envelope. "This isn't all of it, is it?"

"No, no. I kept some." He gave a sad smile.

"Heather had a head full of hair when she was born." He studied Sonya's head. "Lighter than yours. But your eyes—" He held out a hand as though to touch her, then fisted his fingers and dropped his arm. "Your eyes—"

"What about them?" she asked.

"It doesn't matter." He forced a smile and Sonya exchanged a confused look with Brandon. He shrugged. Then Mr. Bradley blurted, "Your eyes look just like hers."

"Do you have a photo?"

"Of course." He walked to the mantel and pulled a small photo from behind another picture. "We don't keep pictures of Heather on display. It's just too painful for my wife." He handed the picture to Sonya. "That's Heather. She's sleeping in that one. If you want one of her awake, I'll have to go find an album."

Sonya stared at the picture, sucked in a breath and let it out slow. The baby looked a lot like some of the pictures she'd seen of herself as an infant. Of course, a lot of babies looked similar when that young. She forced a smile and handed the photo back. "Thank you."

Brandon tucked the envelope into his pants pocket. "We'll let you know something as soon as possible."

"I would appreciate it."

Brandon took her arm and she tried not to notice

how natural and right it felt to walk beside him. How her head came right to his shoulder and how his subtle cologne made her draw in a deep breath and savor the spicy scent. She liked this man, but didn't have any business doing so. However, that didn't seem to matter to her heart. She wanted to get to know him better, find out what made him tick, but knew she shouldn't.

On the other hand, he had secrets, a hardness about his eyes that made her wonder what he'd seen, what he'd lived. Getting behind that wall scared her even while the idea intrigued her.

She shut the thoughts down. Finding out what the baby bag and items were doing in her mother's house was her priority. Romance wasn't even on the table as an option right now.

The thought made her frown.

And then Brandon was holding the car door open for her. She slid in and leaned her head back against the headrest.

"Are you okay?"

"I'm tired. Just plain exhausted." She lifted a hand to her throat. "And sore." She tossed him a weary smile. "But very glad to be alive. If that's all I have to complain about, I'm far better off than some people." She thought about the women in the park. "Far better off."

He smiled back. "I know what you mean. I'll drop you off at home. Frankie's exhausted. I've got a buddy who's going to keep an eye on you while I run this to the lab."

"I'll be fine."

"I want someone with you twenty-four-seven until we find out who's threatening you."

She shivered. "You're right. I think I want that, too." The thought of being alone, being the prey of an unknown stalker who wouldn't hesitate to kill her, filled her with a fear like none she'd ever felt before.

"What about your friend Missy? Would she let you stay with her?"

"I'll text her and see." She glanced at the clock. "It's getting pretty late. Almost ten o'clock." She tapped out the text to Missy and asked if she could stay at her house.

Almost immediately the reply came. Of course. Come on over.

"All right, I'll take you home to get your stuff."

She nodded and felt relieved. Being at Missy's would take a little of the fear away. Having someone else listen for danger would be a big help. "Do you think he's following us? Watching and waiting to strike again? Tonight?"

He glanced in the rearview mirror as he drove and shook his head. "I can't say no, but I've been watching and haven't seen anyone following."

She heard what he left unsaid. Just because he hadn't seen anyone didn't mean no one was there.

She shivered. "I hope your friend can get the results back from the DNA pretty quick."

"Holt's a good guy. He's kind of like me and works all the time. He'll run it for us as soon as he gets a chance. When I drop this off, I'll really stress the necessity for speed."

She studied him. "Why *do* you work all the time, Brandon?"

He shot her a frown. "What do you mean?"

"You just said you work all the time. Do you have any hobbies?"

He shrugged. "Not really. Unless you count the mentoring work I do with at-risk kids."

"Like Spike."

"Yes. Spike's one of them. And I like basketball, but mostly I work."

"Why?"

"Does it matter?"

Well, he knew how to shut a person out, didn't he? To her surprise, she wasn't hurt, just curious.

"Yes. It matters, but you don't have to tell me unless you want to."

"My fiancée left me." His fingers flexed on the wheel as he pulled into her driveway and put the car in Park.

"Oh."

Sitting outside her home, silence descended, blanketing them as completely as the dark of the night. Only a small streetlight provided a bit of light. Enough to see his profile and the wrinkles in his forehead. Then the wrinkles smoothed and he let out a small laugh. "'Oh'? That's it?"

Sonya felt the heat flood her face and was grateful for the darkness. "I'm sorry. I just wasn't expecting you to say that."

"I wasn't, either." He sounded almost bemused.

"Why did she leave you?"

"She found someone who didn't have as much baggage, didn't work as many hours and had money to spend on her." The bemusement was gone. The flat, hard statement told her how much his fiancée had hurt him. "We were supposed to meet for dinner one night. I arrived at the restaurant. She didn't. When I called to see if she was all right, she didn't answer. I went to her house and she was having a candlelit dinner with my accountant."

Silence reigned in the car for a full minute.

"Well..." She drew the word out, thinking of a response.

"Well, what?"

She gave a small shrug and struggled to find the right words. Unable to think of any, she settled on "That really stinks."

More silence, and then he gave another low

chuckle. "Yes. Yes, it does. It did." He finally turned his head toward her and she could see his eyes. Eyes that didn't look hard or flat. Eyes that looked confused and maybe held a hint of surprise.

She gave an embarrassed cluck of her tongue. "That was a dumb response, wasn't it? I'm sorry. I just wasn't sure what to say."

"Your response was absolutely perfect. Most people just offer platitudes or they get embarrassed and don't want to talk about it." He took a deep breath. "Or they tell me they know how I feel and I'll recover with time. That last one is the one that bothers me most."

Puzzled, she cocked her head and frowned at him. "Well, I certainly wouldn't say that. I *don't* know how it feels." She hesitated briefly. "And I don't want to, either," she blurted.

This time he threw his head back and let out a belly laugh. She stared at him, wondering if he'd lost his mind. Then he leaned over and placed his lips on hers. Stunned, she didn't move. The kiss was light, almost like a thank-you, yet with something more, something deeper, something that made her blood hum and her heart sing.

When he lifted his head, he cupped her chin. "You never say what I think you're going to say."

"And you just did something I never expected you to do."

A grin pulled at the corner of his lips. "I really like you, Sonya Daniels."

The present slammed her. She bit her lip. "Sonya Daniels? Or Heather Bradley?"

SEVEN

Brandon sat back with a jerk. What was he doing?

"This is where you apologize, right?" she asked softly.

He sighed. "Apologize? No. I won't apologize for the kiss. I don't know that I can explain it, but I won't apologize for it."

She gave him a slow smile. "Good. And it doesn't need an explanation."

"But we can't let this go anywhere. Not yet."

"What?" she asked.

"Huh?" He blinked.

"Let what go anywhere?"

"This. Us. You know what I'm talking about." He felt the heat creeping into his cheeks. How had he found himself having this awkward conversation? He didn't do awkward. He didn't kiss clients, either.

"Yes, I do." She patted his hand. "Don't worry about it, Brandon. I'm a big girl."

"Sonya—"

"I'm going to get some stuff. I'll be right back."

"I'm coming with you. I don't want you going anywhere alone unless you just absolutely have to."

She climbed from the car and stopped. Stared. "That's weird."

"What is?"

"It's dark and I know I left lights on. You think the power went off?"

He frowned as he took in the house. No porch light, no soft glow coming through the blinds from the inside. Then he glanced around the neighborhood. "Your neighbors have power. Let me take a look."

He placed his hand on his weapon and unsnapped the safety strap. She walked up the front porch and unlocked the door. He slipped around her. "Stay back."

She stayed back. Slightly.

He made his way into the foyer, senses alert to anything that didn't belong. The house smelled of a mixture of lavender and chamomile. Like her.

He moved into the kitchen, feeling her presence right behind him. He didn't hit the light switch, not wanting to be blinded by the sudden brightness. Instead, he let the moon filtering through the kitchen blinds guide his way.

The front door slammed shut.

Sonya let out a yelp and spun to face the noise.

Brandon raced to the door, stood to the side and flipped on the porch light. He looked out, blinking, letting his eyes adjust while he stayed out of the line of fire.

With the door cracked, he listened. Heard a scrape.

He peered around the edge of the doorway, the porch light illuminating all the way to the driveway. Sonya stayed behind him. Good—he wanted to know where she was at all times. His adrenaline pulsed, keeping his senses sharp. Acutely in tune with everything around him, he probed the darkness beyond the reach of the light.

Movement at the back of his car, the trunk area. He lifted his weapon. "Police! Freeze!" The figure obeyed but stayed bent over. "Show me your hands!" The intruder hesitated. "Hands, hands! Show them to me!"

Two gloved hands reached up from behind the trunk. No weapon in sight. Brandon started toward him, his gun held ready, adrenaline pumping through him. Finally, he was going to get the person who didn't want Heather Bradley found.

As he got closer, the intruder darted across the street and into the neighbor's yard. Brandon took three steps to follow then stopped. Sonya raced past him. "Hey!" He shook off his shock and followed her. "What are you doing?"

She didn't answer, just kept up the pursuit. He

trailed hard and fast on her heels, as determined to protect her as she seemed to be to put herself in danger. They were going to have to have a serious talk when he caught up with her.

And then she stopped. Spun in a circle and slapped both palms against her thighs in frustration. "Where'd he go?" He noticed she was barely out of breath. Even after everything she'd been through that evening.

"Are you crazy?" he asked. He drew in a lungful of air and scanned the area. The intruder was gone. At least out of sight. Who knew if he was still watching them? Taking aim?

"I want to know who keeps threatening me. I want to catch him." Frustration filled her voice and she kept clenching and unclenching her fingers.

He gripped her hand and pulled her back toward her house. "Come on. No sense in giving someone a perfect target." Once in the safety of her house, he called it in. Officers were on the way, although what he hoped they'd find, he couldn't say. The person had been dressed in black and wore gloves. If the front porch light hadn't been on, Brandon never would have seen him.

Back inside the house, he looked at Sonya. "What in the world were you thinking, taking off after him like that?"

She ran a hand through her tangled hair. "I

knew you wouldn't chase him if it meant leaving me behind."

He blinked. And stared. She was absolutely right. "So you decided to run after him."

She shrugged and touched her throat with a wince. "I knew you'd be right behind me."

"You're fast."

"I run a lot."

He lifted a brow. "I can tell."

"I wasn't fast enough, though, was I?" she murmured.

"That might not be a bad thing. Don't do that again, okay?" He shuddered to think what might have happened had she actually caught up with the guy. "How's your throat?"

She lifted a hand and touched her throat with a grimace. "It hurts."

Two police cars pulled up, lights flashing. Sonya winced. "Could they at least turn their lights off? All of my neighbors are going to be over here within seconds."

Brandon walked out and flashed his badge. He asked them to douse the lights then started his explanation of what had transpired over the past hour.

Sonya called Missy and let her know she'd be a little late, then went to pack her bags. When she came back into the den, the officers were gone and Brandon thought she looked exhausted. "It's a good thing you don't have to work tomorrow."

"Tell me about it."

"I hope you plan to sleep late. Just in case, I'm still going to have someone watching Missy's house."

She nodded. "Thank you."

The frown between her brows didn't bode well. "What is it?" he asked.

"I'm just wondering if I'm putting Missy at risk by staying with her."

Brandon wanted to reassure her, but he didn't want to tell her anything that wasn't true. He sighed. "I don't know. We're not telling anyone where you're going and we're going to have someone tailing us to make sure you get to Missy's house unobserved."

"Okay. That sounds good." The frown remained.

"What else?"

"What if whoever is after me knows I'm friends with her? The person wouldn't have to follow us. He could just be there waiting for me to show up."

Brandon pursed his lips then blew out a sigh. "Well, that's a possibility, of course, but I'm hoping with the two guys I've got watching you, if anyone is planning any more mayhem, these guys will scare them off."

Again she nodded. "Two guys?"

"Yes. One for the back and one for the front."

"Okay." The frown finally faded.

"So are you ready?"

"I guess so."

He held the door open for her. The two buddies he'd asked to stay on her tonight sat in their vehicles. He pointed to the red truck. "That's Max Powell." She waved. Max waved back. Brandon pointed to the black Explorer. "That's Peter Hayes, my brother."

"Your brother?"

"Yeah. He needed a job and I told him he could help out tonight."

"Oh. Okay. So he works for Finding the Lost on occasion?"

"On occasion. Sort of on an as-needed basis. It's a long story, Sonya. I'll tell you about it one day, but not tonight. Suffice it to say, Peter will do a good job, I promise."

"All right. If you trust him, I trust him."

Her simple faith in him made him swallow hard. He decided to tell her a bit more. "There's a lot of history with Peter. I'll be honest with you. He's a recovering drug addict, but he's been clean for months. He's doing his best to get his life back on track and I want to help him do that."

She shot him a warm smile. "I understand."

Peter got out of his car and walked to the back of Brandon's sedan. He leaned over and picked something up. Studied it.

"What is it?" Brandon asked.

"I'm not sure." He carried the item to the front porch and held it up to the light. "Looks like some sort of wire."

"What made you notice it?"

"When I backed up a little, my headlights swept across it. Thought it might be a nail and didn't want you to pick it up in your tire."

Brandon looked at the wire. Flashed back to the person behind his car. His gut tightened. "I've got a bad feeling about this."

Peter lifted a brow. "Why's that?"

"I need some light."

Sonya set her bag on the ground. "I've got a flashlight in the garage." She hurried to get it while Brandon moved to the back of his vehicle. Peter followed. Max got out of his vehicle. "What's going on, guys?"

Sonya returned with the flashlight. Brandon took it from her. "I want to check under my car. Someone was right behind it. If there's a tracking device, I want it. Or if someone was messing with any wires, I want to know which ones." Brandon stretched out on the driveway behind his car and shone the light underneath it. He looked at his brother. "Do you have a mirror?"

Peter shrugged. "Yeah, in my truck. Hold on a sec." He got it and returned to Brandon, who scooted a little farther under. His gasp jerked Sonya's head up.

"Max?" Brandon said.

"Yeah?"

"Can you take Sonya over to your vehicle and wait a minute?"

Max's gaze sharpened. Without another word, he motioned for Sonya to join him. Confusion on her face, she snagged her bag from the ground and walked over to Max. "What's going on?" She looked from one man to the next.

Peter's hands fisted and he stepped back. "Brandon, what do you see?"

Max gripped her upper arm and gently led her farther away. Brandon maneuvered out from under his vehicle, his face pale in the porch light.

"It's not a tracker."

"What is it?" Sonya asked.

Brandon continued walking toward her. "A bomb. We need a bomb squad."

EIGHT

Sonya watched the bomb squad go to work. She wanted to scream, to give in and promise to quit looking for Heather Bradley. She didn't want people she cared about to be in danger because of her. She looked at the muscle jumping in Brandon's jaw and knew even if she decided to stop looking, he wouldn't.

The twitching muscle, narrowed eyes and hands on his hips shouted his determination to figure out who had just tried to blow him—them—up.

The clock pushed eleven-thirty and she texted Missy and told her friend to just go on to bed. Missy told her where to find the key, but made her promise to tell her everything in the morning.

Sonya agreed, but wondered if she'd even make it to her friend's house by morning. At this rate, she didn't know if she'd even be alive come morning. She swallowed hard and forced those thoughts from her mind. "Please, Lord, let us figure out who Heather Bradley is and who doesn't want us to know. I really don't want to die over this."

The whispered prayer echoed through her mind even as she walked over to hear Brandon ask, "How would it be detonated? It was under the back of the car. The person didn't have time to attach anything to the ignition."

"It wasn't going to go off until the person wanted it to."

"Remote detonation?"

"Yeah."

Brandon cocked his head. "I don't understand. We were all standing around the car at one point. Whoever had the remote could have blown us all to our final reward."

The bomb-squad member held up two wires. "These weren't attached. In order for the bomb to be remotely accessed, these wires have to be attached. My guess is you scared him off before he got them connected." He shook his head. "You guys are one lucky group."

Sonya swallowed hard. "I don't really care why. I think I'll just be grateful it didn't go off."

"I sure would be."

The man walked away and Brandon stepped over to Sonya. She looked up at him, thankful he was still here with her. She moved toward him and wrapped her arms around his waist and hugged him. He patted her back and gave her a hug. She stepped back. "Please don't ever put yourself in danger like that again."

He sighed. "I didn't realize I was in any danger until I saw the bomb." He paused. "And I guess I wasn't really in any danger if the bomb wasn't going to go off. Sure spiked my adrenaline when I saw it, though."

Neighbors crowded their porches and people moved into the street to get a better view of the happenings at her house. Sonya groaned. Just what she needed. An audience and an endless parade of neighbors with offers of help. Not that she didn't appreciate their kindness, but—

"Sonya?"

She turned. Doris Talbot. Her mother's best friend. The woman barely topped five feet and she was as wide as she was tall. Her heart was just as big and Sonya loved her dearly. She walked over and gave the woman a hug, inhaling the scent of mountain-fresh fabric softener and Pine-Sol. "Hi." This was one neighbor she didn't mind seeing.

"Honey, what's going on?"

"It's a really long story."

Mrs. Talbot glanced around at the flashing lights and milling law-enforcement officers. "I'll say." Her gaze lasered in on Sonya's throat. "What happened to you?"

"I had a little incident at work." Sonya had an

idea. "Mrs. Talbot, did my mother ever say anything to you about a baby named Heather Bradley?"

"Heather Bradley?" She wrinkled her brow. "No, not that I recall. Why?"

Sonya forced a smile. "No reason. Mom just seemed really upset in her last few days and I can't figure out why."

"And you think a baby had something to do with it?"

"Maybe." Sonya sighed. It was late and Mrs. Talbot had sweat dripping into her eyes. As much as she'd like to continue questioning the woman, she knew she had heart issues. Being out in this humid heat and all the excitement of having law enforcement practically in her backyard probably wasn't good for her. She placed a hand on the woman's upper arm. "Why don't we talk tomorrow? I can explain a little more then."

"That's fine. What time? I'll make a dessert."

Sonya mentally went through her day tomorrow. She didn't have to work, but she did have to pick up her car. "Now, don't go to any trouble." She knew she would regardless of the admonishment. "How about we make it lunch? I'll pick up some sandwiches. My treat."

The older woman's eyes lit up. "That sounds lovely."

Sonya gave her another hug. "Why don't you go

home and cool off? All of the excitement around here is getting ready to come to an end anyway."

"Oh, yes. What happened?"

Sonya hesitated. "I thought I saw someone lurking outside my house." No way was she going to tell the woman about the bomb under Brandon's car. If she didn't recognize the bomb-squad vehicle, Sonya wasn't going to fill her in.

"What?" Mrs. Talbot placed a hand against her chest. "Oh, my. How dreadful. I won't sleep a wink tonight."

Sonya sighed. "Really, I don't think you have a thing to worry about. Please, get some rest. You're not in any danger. If there was someone here, he's long gone by now."

Mrs. Talbot looked uncertain. Then she gave a slow nod. "Guess I'll just have to trust the good Lord to keep me safe, eh?"

"Exactly." *Trust in the Lord with all your heart...*

"All right, I'll see you tomorrow, dear."

"Tomorrow."

Mrs. Talbot waddled home and Sonya turned to find Brandon watching her. He smiled. "You ready to go to Missy's?"

"Yes, but I have one question."

"What's that?"

"You've got people who are going to be watching out for Missy and me, but who's going to be watching out for you?"

He trailed a gentle finger down her cheek and she shivered at the heat his touch evoked. "You don't need to worry about me. I can take care of myself."

"Not if someone decides to blow you up," she said. She knew it was blunt, but the fact remained that less than thirty minutes ago he'd had a bomb under his car.

He nodded. "Good point. But now that I know the attacks aren't limited to just you, I'll be more aware and on guard."

Sonya ran a hand through her hair and sighed. "Okay." She told him about having lunch with her neighbor tomorrow.

He nodded. "Do you mind if I join you?"

"Of course I don't mind." She gave him a small smile. "But I'll warn you. Mrs. Talbot is an outrageous flirt. Anytime there's a good-looking man around, her flirt radar is triggered."

His lips tipped upward. "So you think I'm good-looking?"

Sonya felt the heat arrive in her cheeks with a rush. "Um…well. Uh…sure."

He laughed. A laugh so full of amusement that it caught the attention of the other men. Peter raised a brow and Max sent a bemused grin in their direction.

Sonya allowed her own grin to spread. "Oh,

wow, you really took advantage of that one, didn't you?"

"Sorry. I couldn't resist." Brandon snickered one more time, then traced her lips with a finger. "Now, that is a genuine smile."

A sweet tingling sensation spread through her. She snapped her lips together, but knew her eyes still held her laughter. He snagged her fingers with his. "Come on. I'll take you to Missy's."

The lighthearted moment felt strange given the seriousness of the situation, but she needed it. Desperately. Even though she was a tad embarrassed. Still, she could laugh at herself and decided that was a good thing. When he met Mrs. Talbot tomorrow, he wouldn't be laughing so hard.

But she probably would be.

Brandon walked into the office at seven-thirty the next morning. He found his sergeant, Christine Adams, drinking a cup of coffee and staring at the fax machine. His boss was a short woman, not more than five feet two inches, with dark brown hair she wore pulled up in a bun. She wore her makeup like body armor and he'd never seen her without it. "You have a minute, Sarge?"

Christine lowered her mug and lifted her dark eyes from the machine. "I guess standing here isn't going to get me the information any faster. Come on in my office."

Brandon followed her and shut the door behind him. Christine took a seat behind her desk and motioned him to one of the vacant chairs along the opposite wall, where he sat. "What's up?"

Brandon leaned back and crossed his legs. "I guess you heard about the excitement last night?"

"Some of it. Someone planted a bomb on your car?"

"Exactly."

"Who are you making mad?"

"Good question."

Christine pursed her lips and steepled her fingers in front of her as she studied him. "You need some time?"

"I think I do."

"I think you may be right. Someone planting a bomb on your vehicle is pretty serious stuff. Nothing to play around with."

"That's kind of the way I feel about it."

She nodded. "What can we do to help?"

He shrugged. "Hector said he'd cover our cases for me. If he needs help, it would be good to have another detective available."

"We can do that. What else?"

"Can I let you know as things come up?"

"Of course." Christine frowned. "Keep me updated, Brandon. You're a good detective and I don't want to lose you."

"Thanks, I appreciate it. And the time."

She nodded. Her phone rang and she lifted a hand to wave. His dismissal. He didn't take it personally. He liked Christine and respected her. She was good at her job and she took care of her detectives. He appreciated that.

Brandon went to his office and found Hector at his desk. "I'm taking off a few days."

"If someone planted a bomb on my car, I would, too."

"That's not the only reason, but I'm going to need your help."

"You name it."

Brandon sat down. "You got a minute?"

"All day."

"Then I want to tell you what's going on."

For the next few minutes, Brandon brought his partner up to speed on everything that had happened from the time Sonya had walked into his office until he'd found the bomb under his car.

Hector shook his head. "And you have no idea who this Heather Bradley is?"

"Just that she was kidnapped as an infant."

"And you think Sonya Daniels is Heather."

"Maybe. She looks like Don Bradley and favors Ann a bit." He shrugged. "I dropped some samples off at the lab, so I'm still waiting for the results."

"What's your gut feeling?"

"My gut says she's Heather Bradley and the kidnapper knows she's back."

NINE

Sonya rolled over and pulled the covers over her head. Then smelled coffee and sat up. She could hear Missy in the kitchen, humming a tuneless melody. Her entire body ached. She touched her throat and grimaced. The stitches felt hot and uncomfortable, but nothing a couple of ibuprofen tablets couldn't handle.

After a quick shower and an abbreviated morning routine, she made her way into the kitchen.

Missy sat at the table, her steaming mug and Bible in front of her. She looked up and smiled. "Morning."

"Hey."

"Coffee's over there."

"Thanks."

Sonya poured herself a cup and popped two pieces of bread into the toaster.

"Are you going to tell me what happened last night or keep me in suspense until I simply burst?"

Sonya gave a small laugh, then quickly sobered.

"How long did the police stay at the hospital questioning people after I left?"

"Forever. Now, what happened?"

When Sonya finished her recap of the day's events, Missy stared wide-eyed, jaw hanging. Sonya sighed. "So now I don't know whether I should stay here or not. I probably need to figure something else out."

"Absolutely not."

Sonya looked at her friend. "I appreciate your willingness to let me stay, but I won't put you in danger."

"I'm not giving you a choice. You're staying right here." She got up and walked to the window and looked out. "And cool. We have our own personal bodyguards."

"Missy, I don't think you understand. This person wasn't playing around. He put a bomb under Brandon's car."

Missy frowned. "I know. I get that, but I still think you'd be safer here with me than off on your own somewhere. Just stay, okay?"

"I wouldn't necessarily be on my own, but—"

"Good. Then it's settled."

Sonya blinked. "Missy—"

"Now, what are you going to do all day?" She narrowed her eyes at the wound on Sonya's neck. "You should probably rest. Have you taken your antibiotic?"

Sonya sighed. "Yes, I took it this morning. And I'm meeting my neighbor for lunch to talk to her about anything my mother may have said to her before she died."

"Well, sounds like a plan. I'm going to baby-sit my four-year-old niece while my sister goes to have her hair done. Will you text me throughout the day and let me know you're all right?"

Sonya's heart warmed. It was nice to have someone who cared. "Sure. And thanks."

"No worries."

"But the minute it looks like you're being targeted because of your association with me, I'm out of here, okay?"

"Okay. Now hush and let me finish my quiet time."

Sonya smiled and took a sip of her coffee, fixed her toast with the apple butter she found in the fridge and went into the den. Having a quiet time sounded like a wonderful idea.

At eleven-thirty, Brandon pulled up in front of Missy's house. He waved to Peter, who'd stayed most of the night and insisted on taking the morning hours until Brandon's arrival. Now he'd go home to sleep and be ready for more duty if Brandon needed him later.

He opened the door to step out at the same time Sonya opened the front door. She must have been waiting for him. He climbed out and went around to open the passenger door for her. "Good morning." He noticed the hint of vanilla when she stepped close to him. The sun picked up the red highlights in her hair. Hair that looked soft and silky and made him itch to run his fingers through it.

"Hi. Thanks for picking me up."

He balled his fingers into fists and told himself to stop. She was off-limits. For now. "No problem."

"I'm guessing you checked under your car this morning?"

He gave a short laugh. "Trust me, I went over it with a fine-tooth comb."

"Good."

"And when we go to pick yours up, I'll do the same."

His statement silenced her for a brief moment. Then she rubbed her forehead. "I didn't even think about that."

"That's what I'm here for."

She reached over and took his hand in hers and squeezed. "And I want you to know how very thankful I am for that."

Her words shattered part of the wall around his heart, and he tightened his hand around hers even while his mind screamed at him to put the distance back, push her away. He cleared his throat. "That's why you're paying me the big bucks, right?"

She slipped her hand away from his, and he had no trouble discerning her cooling attitude. "Of course." She paused. "Do you mind swinging by the Sandwich Factory? I told Mrs. Talbot I'd bring sandwiches."

"Sonya, I—"

She turned her head to look out the window, effectively cutting him off. He wanted to kick himself. He hadn't meant to hurt her, but in fear of his growing feelings for her, his desperate need to put some space between them, he'd done just that.

He pulled away from the curb and drew in a deep breath. More vanilla. And coffee. He wondered if she liked cream and sugar in it or drank it black.

"Thank you for arranging protection last night," she said, her tone neutral.

"You're welcome. I'm just glad the rest of the night was uneventful."

She blew out a breath and turned back toward him. "Me, too." Her frostiness had melted slightly, as though she'd made up her mind not to be mad at him.

"I'd stay and watch each night if I didn't need to be alert during the day. Peter's a night owl anyway. He can go home and sleep."

"So tell me about your family. There's Peter. And I know Erica's your sister. Any other siblings?"

"No." He heard his curt tone, but couldn't seem to help it. Talking about his family ranked number one on his least-favorite-things-to-do list.

This time his snappy reply didn't seem to faze her. "I got the feeling you were close to Erica."

"I am."

"And you give your brother a job when he needs one. But you don't like talking about your family."

So she'd noticed.

Relief filled him as he pulled into the parking lot of the Sandwich Factory. She shot him a thin smile. "I'll be right back."

"I'm coming with you." He didn't want her walking in alone. They'd told no one their destination, but he still wanted to stay close to her.

Together, they walked into the restaurant. She stood in line and Brandon watched her watch others. She'd become more alert, more aware of her surroundings since walking into his office two weeks ago. He was glad and pained at the same time. The line moved fast, and since she'd called the order in, they were back in the car within minutes. Sonya settled the bag at her feet.

Brandon glanced around, his senses sharp. Had they been followed? There'd been no indication anyone had been behind them, but he didn't let that stop him from being on the alert.

"Family's always been very important to me." She picked up right where she'd left off and he gave a silent groan. "The possibility of finding out that my parents aren't really my parents is scary. And incredibly hurtful. I have so many great memories with them. I just can't picture them doing anything illegal like adopting a kidnapped child."

He could imagine. He'd also hoped the whole family topic had been shelved. But it hadn't. Sonya was obviously still thinking about their previous conversation. Personally, he wouldn't mind finding out he had another set of parents somewhere, but didn't figure he'd voice that thought. "That's understandable."

He could feel her gaze boring into him. "What would you do if you were in my shoes?"

He didn't answer right away. In fact, he thought long and hard about it. She seemed to understand that he was thinking and didn't rush his answer. Finally, he said, "I would wait until I had all the facts before I made any decisions one way or another. If the DNA results come back that you're not related to Heather Bradley, then you can probably rest easy that you're not adopted."

"And if they come back saying otherwise?"

He sighed. "Then I suppose you'll have to deal with it, but until we know for sure, let's just focus on the facts."

"Which are?"

"Someone doesn't want us finding Heather Bradley and is willing to go to extreme lengths to keep us from looking for her."

"But who? Who benefits from us not finding her?"

"The only person I can think of is the person who kidnapped her."

"Agreed." She thought about it. "What about their adopted son? I mean, the Bradleys have a lot of money. What if he feels threatened? Like, if I'm proven to be Heather, he'll have to split the inheritance." She shook her head. "He wouldn't, though. I don't care about their money. I just want the truth."

He nodded. "I thought about that. I've got my partner, Hector, looking into him in addition to anyone who was close to the family at the time Heather disappeared."

"Why do you think it was someone close?"

"Heather disappeared from the church nursery. Whoever took her is someone who fit in at the church and didn't stand out in any way. I read the report and all of the interviews done the day of the kidnapping. It was really pretty thorough. No one reported seeing anyone strange that Sunday. No one who made them stop twice for a second look."

"What about visitors?"

"The church was the largest one in town. They had visitors every Sunday. Visitors had the option to fill out a visitor card—or not. So even if we had a list of everyone who attended that day, there's no guarantee the person who took Heather filled anything out."

"No, the kidnapper wouldn't have wanted to leave any kind of trace. And if it was someone in the church, he—or she—would have known about the visitor cards."

"Right. So, Hector's looking into Mr. Bradley's business connections back then. See if anything makes a blip on the radar." He turned onto Mrs. Talbot's street and Sonya looked over at her mother's house. Now hers. It looked absolutely normal with no sign of the drama that had played out last night.

He parked the car and Mrs. Talbot stepped out onto her front porch, a wide smile of greeting on her lined face. She waved. "Come on in. I've got desserts all ready for after the sandwiches."

"Desserts?" he whispered.

"She's a baker. Trust me, you'll love anything she puts in front of you."

His mouth started watering before his foot hit the first step.

Sonya stepped inside the familiar foyer and her throat clogged with tears. As a child, she'd grown up about an hour and a half away, but her mother had always loved Spartanburg, having lived here until she met Sonya's father.

Throughout Sonya's childhood, they'd made trips to visit, always stopping to see Mrs. Talbot, who became like a grandmother to Sonya. Sonya's mother and Mrs. Talbot might have had a twenty-year age difference, but they'd been tight friends.

When the house across the street had come up for sale, shortly after Sonya had gone off to college, her father had purchased it and her parents moved home. Sonya finished undergraduate school, then graduate. One semester away from fulfilling her dream of becoming a doctor, she'd come home to take care of her mother.

A woman who might not be her mother.

Sonya introduced Brandon to the woman. Mrs. Talbot grinned. "So, you're Sonya's young man, are you?"

Brandon lifted a brow and glanced at Sonya. She knew her face was three different shades of red. "No, Mrs. Talbot, we're…friends," she answered before Brandon had a chance to say anything. No sense in going into everything right now.

"Well, if you're not smart enough to snag him, I might have a go at it." She winked at Brandon and turned toward the kitchen, fingers clutched around the sandwich bag. "Handsome thing like that, girl's got no sense if she's not going after that one…." She disappeared into the kitchen.

Sonya sighed and shook her head. "I told you."

Brandon grinned. "This is going to be interesting, isn't it?"

"You have no idea." He shut the door behind them, but not before she saw him take a look down the street, first to the right, then to the left. "See anything?"

The door snicked closed. "No."

"But you think someone followed us?"

"I don't know. I just want to be careful not to let my guard down."

She nodded. "I'm going to help Mrs. Talbot."

"I'm going to watch the street."

Sonya frowned. "All right." His vigilance hit home. The niggling thought that she might be putting the older woman in danger just by being in her house wouldn't leave her alone. Sonya decided they probably needed to eat and talk and get out as fast as they could without being rude.

Mrs. Talbot hummed as she worked, setting the sandwiches on her fine china. "Why don't you pour the tea, child?"

Sonya smiled. She'd always be a child to this dear lady. She did as instructed. "Do you mind if I ask you a couple of strange questions?"

"Strange questions?"

"About my mother."

Grief flashed across Mrs. Talbot's face. "No,

I don't mind. I love talking about your mother. Goodness, I do miss that woman."

"I know." Sonya swallowed against the instant tears. "I miss her, too."

"Your father, too. He was such a good man. Loved your mother and you like I've never seen before. Would have done anything for the two of you."

"Yes, I know. Daddy was a wonderful man."

Mrs. Talbot cocked her head toward the den area, where Brandon was. "That one got potential?"

Sonya refused to blush. "He's helping me with something."

"What's that?"

"I found something in Mom's closet when I was going through her house, getting it ready for the estate sale."

Mrs. Talbot paused and studied her. "Something that has you troubled. What was it?"

"A baby bag with a birth certificate."

"Yours?"

"No. It belonged to a baby named Heather Bradley. Did Mom ever say anything about it?"

"No, she never did."

"You saw her in her last days. Did you notice how troubled she was?"

A sigh slipped from the woman's lips. "Well,

truth be told, I did notice she seemed fairly agitated, but I thought she was just in pain."

She had been in pain, of course. "I think it was more than the physical pain of her disease. I think it was something else."

"Like what?"

Frustration filled Sonya. "Like something was on her mind and troubling her." She sighed. "I wish I knew."

"And I wish I could help you, honey, but I can't recall anything. She never said a word to me about anything that was troubling her. Other than leaving you, of course. She hated to leave you."

Sonya's throat closed and she fought the tears that wanted to flow.

Mrs. Talbot motioned toward the table. "Call your young man in here and let's eat."

Sonya nodded and took a deep breath. She wouldn't cry. She didn't have time for tears. If she could stay focused on the goal of finding out about the baby bag and Heather Bradley, she would be all right.

Throughout lunch, Sonya asked question after question and finally realized she wasn't going to get any more information from Mrs. Talbot. Although she had to admit watching Brandon gently field the woman's flirtatious comments was quite amusing.

He even thrilled Mrs. Talbot by flirting back a

bit. Lighthearted and innocent, the woman giggled like a schoolgirl. Sonya thought it was charming and sweet and said a lot about Brandon's true personality. She found herself drawn even more to the man.

When Mrs. Talbot wasn't flirting, she enjoyed reminiscing and telling stories about Sonya's mother, but repeated that she had no idea about Heather Bradley or what her friend might have been so agitated about in the last few weeks of her life.

Brandon and Sonya left with promises to visit again soon. Sonya climbed into Brandon's car and shut the door.

He slipped in beside her. "She's quite a character, isn't she?"

"That's putting it mildly, but I love her."

"I can see why. I wonder if my siblings and I would have turned out different if we'd had someone like her in our lives."

His personal comment made her pause. "What do you mean?"

He flushed. "Nothing. It's not important."

She huffed. "Is it just me? Or do you shut everyone out?"

He stiffened. "I don't shut everyone out."

"Okay."

He drove for the next few minutes in silence. "I don't."

"Okay."

He tapped the wheel with his hands and hummed an eighties tune she recognized, but couldn't name. He stopped humming. "Do I?"

"Yes."

"Oh." Another long pause. "I'm sorry."

She shrugged. "I think it's just become a habit with you."

He didn't answer and she looked at him, ready to repeat the statement, but the look on his face stopped her. He was staring into the mirror, eyes narrowed, jaw tight. "What is it?" she asked.

"We've got company and I don't think it's the good kind."

TEN

Brandon sped up.

"Who is it? Can you see?"

"No, but he's been on us since we turned out of your subdivision."

"You think he saw us leave Mrs. Talbot's?"

"I'm not sure. I don't think so. I think he was waiting at the entrance."

She turned to look out the back. "It's a brown sedan. Very nondescript."

The car continued to close in. Brandon sped up. The sedan backed off.

"Wish I could see the license plate."

Brandon pulled his phone from the cup holder and called in the description of the vehicle. The car stayed with them as he came to a red light. "I'm going to stop and see what he does. Duck down."

"But—"

"Just do it," he snapped.

Sonya flinched and unclipped her seat belt. She slid down half on the seat, halfway on the floorboard, her brown eyes never leaving his face. He swallowed. He'd been too sharp. In a soft tone he said, "There's a police cruiser just thirty seconds away. He'll be here before I stop at the light."

He hoped.

Brandon pressed the brake and slowed. The sedan stayed on his tail.

Closer. And the vehicle came to a smooth stop just behind his bumper.

Blue lights flashed almost immediately behind the sedan. The driver opened the door and shoved his hands upward.

And Brandon realized who it was. "You can get back up, Sonya. Sorry I snapped at you."

"Who is it?" she asked as she maneuvered back into the seat.

"Spike."

"Spike? What's he doing?"

Brandon threw open his door. "That's what I'm going to find out."

He walked back to the young man, who looked a lot more stressed than the last time he'd seen him just a couple of days ago at the restaurant. The officers from the cruiser had stepped out and approached Spike, hands on their weapons. Brandon waved them off. "Sorry, guys. False alarm."

The officer relaxed. "You sure?" Brandon thought he recognized the man who spoke. Jason Newman, a rookie, but one with promise.

"I'm sure. I've got this."

The officers climbed back into their vehicle and left. Brandon turned to Spike, who still had his hands in the air. "Get out of the car, man. What in the world are you doing?"

Spike stood, eyes lowered. "Looking for you."

"You couldn't use a cell phone like usual?"

He shook his head. "I couldn't pay the bill."

"Ah. Okay, then, a friend's phone?"

Another negative.

"Tell me why you're looking for me."

"My mama's sick and I can't afford her medicine."

Brandon got it now.

"Get in the car and follow me to the drugstore."

Spike's head jerked up and his gaze met Brandon's. "I ain't takin' no charity, dude. My mama would have a fit."

Brandon understood the pride behind the token protest. "You don't have to tell her how you paid for it."

Spike's eyes drifted over Brandon's left shoulder. "You're with her again."

"Yes."

He nodded. "Never mind."

"I trust her."

Spike paused. "For real or you playin' me?"

"For real."

"All right, then."

"You lead. I'll follow."

Brandon climbed back in the car and waited for the light to turn green. Their small drama in the street had backed up traffic, although once the other officers left, the cars had started to go around them.

Spike passed him and Brandon fell in behind him.

"What's going on?" Sonya asked.

"I'm doing a favor for a friend." He explained about Spike's mother. "She's got sickle cell and can't afford her medicine. I once told Spike, if he ever found himself in a situation where he needed help, to ask me. He doesn't have any money for the medicine."

"So you gave it to him?"

"No, I'm following him to the pharmacy to buy it for him."

"He's a recovering addict?"

"Yeah. He's been clean for about a year. The medicine's expensive. If I put that much money in his hands, he might be tempted to spend it elsewhere. I won't do that and he knows it." He felt Sonya's eyes on him and it made him a tad uncomfortable. "What?"

"You're a good man, aren't you?"

Now Brandon just felt embarrassed. "I don't know about good, but helping a kid when he needs it seems to be the right thing to do."

"Whatever you do for the least of these," she murmured.

He caught the words and gave her a smile.

Thirty minutes later, Spike had the medicine, three burgers, a large fries and a chocolate shake. He also had a full tank of gas and two bags of groceries, thanks to Brandon's generosity. It wasn't the first time satisfaction filled him after helping someone like Spike. Not from a sense of pride, but from knowing Spike would have a good night and his mother would have her meds.

Brandon hadn't had anyone do that for him when he'd been Spike's age, and he'd vowed if he ever found a way to help kids who couldn't help themselves, he'd do it.

His phone rang. "Hello?"

"Where are you, man?" It was Hector.

"On Calhoun. Why?"

"Can you come down to the station? We've got some video from one of your lady's neighbors. He called us and said he thought he got a picture of the guy who was sneaking around Sonya's house. Even has him at the trunk of your car. It's grainy and fuzzy and the guy has on a hat, so it's probably a long shot, but…"

His lady? What was it with everyone throwing him and Sonya together? First Mrs. Talbot with her "your young man" stuff, now Hector? But he was surprised to find he really didn't mind that much. He'd set Hector straight later. Maybe. "We'll be there in a few minutes." He hung up.

"What is it?" Sonya asked.

"Do you mind coming down to the police station? Hector got a picture from one of your neighbors' security cameras." He paused. "Who would have that kind of security?"

"Mr. Lehman," she answered without hesitation. "He's a retired police officer and his house is wired to the nth degree. He lives directly across the street from me. He has cameras pointed toward the street, which would cover my house. He also has them aimed up and down the street." She slapped her head. "I can't believe I didn't think to ask him about it."

"He called and volunteered it."

"Well, good. Maybe we'll finally see who it is."

"Hector said it isn't a very good picture."

"Well, it won't hurt to look."

Ten minutes later, they walked into the police station. Brandon waved back at those who acknowledged him, but led Sonya straight to his and Hector's desks. The station was a big open room. Desks and phones took up most of the space.

Hector looked up. When his eyes landed on Sonya, his brows lifted and he gave Brandon a thumbs-up. Brandon ground his molars and gave his partner a look that should have sent him scurrying. Instead, Hector grinned. Brandon noticed

Sonya's lack of attention and sent up a silent prayer of thanks that she'd missed the communication between him and Hector. Her head swiveled on her neck and he realized she'd never been in a police station before. "It can be a little overwhelming. Just stick with me."

"Right."

She settled in the chair next to his desk. Brandon introduced her to Hector, who held her hand a few seconds too long, in his opinion. Hector loved women and women loved Hector. Brandon scowled when Sonya smiled prettily. But it wasn't flirty. He breathed deep and tried to resist the sudden flashes of memory. His ex-fiancée telling him she was seeing someone else. Then after they'd split, running into her with her new man at a restaurant and trying to pretend he was all right.

It had hurt.

But looking at Sonya now, he realized it didn't hurt as bad as it had a year ago.

"Bran?"

Hector's voice cut through the memories and he saw they were staring at him. "Oh, right. Sorry. I was thinking about something."

Hector made a humming noise in his throat and let his gaze bounce between Sonya and him. Then he said nothing more, just grabbed a photo from his desk and handed it to Sonya. "Anything look familiar?"

She squinted at the photo, tilted her head and sighed. "No."

"Didn't think you'd get much from it."

She pointed. "Look, there's a smudge—or something—on his right shoulder. Where his shirt slipped down a bit, you can see it. Is that a tattoo?"

Brandon leaned in. "Possibly." He looked at Hector. "Can we get that area enlarged?"

"We can, but it may blur it right out."

"Let's try."

"All right. It'll take a little while to get it back."

Brandon nodded. "I'll put a call in to the lab and request a rush." Hector laughed and Brandon shrugged. "Hey, it can't hurt."

"Brandon?"

He turned to see Mary Ann Delaney, one of the station's secretaries, waving at him. "Yes?"

"You have a visitor."

"A visitor?" He frowned. "Who?"

"Your mother."

Sonya saw him freeze. Saw him go totally still for a full five seconds as a woman with red hair headed toward him. She had a trim figure and green eyes that sparkled.

"That's your mother?" she asked.

"Yes."

"Wow, she's beautiful. She looks more like your sister than your mother."

His eyes shuttered and his lips thinned. "That's

what happens when your mother's only sixteen years older than you are. She's in her mid-forties." His even, flat tone gave nothing—and everything—away.

"Oh." She cleared her throat. "Could you tell me where the nearest ladies' room is?"

He shot her a grateful look. "We passed it on our way in. There on the left." He pointed and she slipped inside before mother and son greeted each other.

Sonya decided to take advantage of the time and wound up retouching what little makeup she wore, and then she brushed her hair and washed her hands.

In the midst of drying her hands, the door opened and two female officers stepped inside. "Can you believe it?"

"She has some nerve showing up here."

"I heard she and her husband are still married, but they abandoned the children when they were younger. Now she's wanting to cozy up and make nice."

The two women talked as though Sonya were invisible.

"I don't see Brandon putting up with that for long. The last time she showed up, he was real quick to show her the door."

Sonya's ears perked up at Brandon's name.

"I don't know, Olivia." The woman paused to

check her makeup in the mirror. Sonya was starting to feel like a fifth wheel. "Brandon's his own person. He's not going to let his mommy run his life, but it looks like she might be wearing him down."

"I didn't say she was trying to run his life. It just seems to me she's pushing for something that's not going to happen. I don't think she's wearing him down at all." The woman stepped into one of the vacant stalls, still talking.

Okay, that was it. Sonya couldn't stand here and listen to them spout their gossip any longer.

Olivia patted her nose. "I think she's just after him because he's a success. He's slightly famous around here and she wants a piece of the status."

"What status?" Sonya blurted.

The officer paused in her reapplication of lip gloss and stared at Sonya as though seeing her for the first time. Sonya thought police officers were supposed to be observant. Honestly.

The officer said, "Excuse me?"

"Brandon is a friend and I don't think he'd appreciate your speculation on his family relationships. No offense, but it's not really your business unless he makes it so." She held up a hand to forestall the woman's words. "And your conversation wasn't my business, either. Sorry for butting in."

But she really wasn't.

She opened the door and stepped out without

another word, heart beating so fast she was afraid it might leap out of her chest. She'd never done anything like that before in her life.

A small smile slipped across her lips. But she had to admit, it had felt good. And right.

The next words she heard wiped the smile off her lips.

"I said no, Mom. Now drop it."

Brandon's cold tone was enough to send shivers up her spine.

"But, son—"

"I've got work to do. Let me walk you out."

Sonya bit her lip as she watched Brandon take his mother's elbow and direct her toward the exit. Hector blew out a sigh. "One day he's going to have to forgive them."

"Who?" she asked.

"His parents." He snapped his lips closed then said, "But you didn't hear that from me."

"Seems like I'm hearing a lot of stuff today," she murmured.

"You're what?"

She glanced at him. "Nothing."

Brandon came back into the building and headed for his desk. Tension radiated from him and Sonya hated it for him. "Goodness, he has some real issues with his family, doesn't he?"

Hector shot her a sharp look. "If you grew up with his parents, you would, too."

"I wasn't being critical," she apologized.

He shrugged. "I was being defensive." He looked at his partner, who'd stopped to speak to another officer. "And he doesn't need my defense. He can handle it himself."

"He doesn't talk about his family much."

"No, he doesn't. It's a topic he avoids, and if you value your hide, you'll stay away from it, too."

Sonya simply watched the man she was starting to care way too much for. She wanted to know what his childhood had been like. She wanted to know how he'd risen up and become a respected citizen, a decorated cop. But that was for him to tell her. She might be curious, but she wouldn't listen to gossip. She wanted the facts from him.

He finally broke away and came back to his desk.

"Are you all right?" she asked.

He pinched the bridge of his nose and shook his head. "I'm fine. Personal stuff that shouldn't happen in the office. She knows I don't appreciate her showing up like that."

Sonya frowned. "Then why would she do it?"

"No worries, my friend," Hector said before Brandon had to answer. He waved the photo and changed the subject. "So we've got a suspect who has a mark on his shoulder."

"Right."

"Fuzzy enough not to be able to make it out, but

we'll give the guys who like to play with photos a chance to clear it up a bit."

"Great." Brandon still looked as if his attention was elsewhere. Then he gave a visible shake and rolled his shoulders as though pushing off the stress his mother's appearance had put him under. "All right. Here's the deal——" His phone rang. He glanced at the screen then at Sonya. "It's Holt, my buddy at the lab."

"Oh, good," she breathed.

"Hello?"

He listened and Sonya strained to hear what Holt was saying, but couldn't catch a word. Brandon nodded. "All right, thanks for letting me know. And thanks for staying late to run the tests. We appreciate it."

He hung up and looked at Sonya. She gulped. "He did the DNA test, didn't he? And got the results?"

"He did."

"And?"

"You and Heather Bradley are a one hundred percent match," he said.

ELEVEN

Brandon watched her absorb the news. He couldn't say he was especially surprised. Not after seeing her next to Don Bradley.

Sonya pulled in a deep breath. "All right, so what does that mean? The parents I grew up with stole me?" Her jaw hardened. "I don't believe it."

"It could be they had no idea you were a kidnapped child. It could be you were a black-market baby. Someone kidnapped you and sold you to the highest bidder, so to speak." Brandon spoke gently. She'd had a shock. And while it looked as though she was dealing with it, he knew she was in for some rough times ahead. He found himself wanting to be there for her. He reached around the desk and took her hand. It trembled in his.

Tears hovered on her lashes, but didn't fall. "So. I'm Heather Bradley. I guess the next step is to let the Bradleys know, right?"

"Yes." He picked his phone up from the desk. "I'll call Don and ask him if we can meet."

She nodded and sniffed. "Today. I want to do it today. If he has the time."

"I'd rather tell him in person. Over the phone seems pretty cold."

"Yes. In person is probably best."

Hector tapped his pen against his desk. "Do you want me to look into your parents' past? See if I can find any record of adoption or how they came to have you?"

Brandon saw a flurry of emotions cross her face, and then she nodded. "Yes. I've come this far. I might as well find out the whole story." She twisted the strap on her purse. "If I don't, I'll just wonder."

"I'll take care of it." Hector made a few notes. "Also, I would think you would want to do DNA tests with the Bradleys."

Sonya blinked. "Why?"

"For their peace of mind, for one thing. Just for extra confirmation."

Brandon dialed the number. Don picked up on the first ring. "Hello?"

"Hello, Don. Brandon Hayes here. I was wondering if you'd have some time to speak with us again."

"I'm at my office. Could you come here?"

"Of course. What time?"

"Anytime."

"We're on our way."

"You have some news, don't you?" He asked the question hesitantly.

"Yes."

"All right." Now the man sounded downright nervous. "I'll be waiting."

Brandon hung up. "All right, let's go."

Sonya stood. "I'm ready."

Hector held up a hand. "Hold on a sec." He had his phone pressed to his ear, listening. He nodded and hung up. "I ran down the Bradleys' son, Donald Junior. He's an accountant for Grand National Bank in Texas. He's been at a conference in San Diego for the past three days. He flies home tomorrow."

"Is he really there?" Brandon asked.

"He's there. He's one of the main speakers and hasn't missed a session."

"Then he's not the one after me," Sonya mused.

"Unless he paid someone," Brandon muttered. He looked at Hector. "Thanks."

"Sure thing."

Brandon escorted her down to where he'd parked the car and helped her in. She had her seat belt fastened by the time he climbed behind the wheel. "Are you all right?"

She let out a sigh. "I'm stunned, Brandon. My brain is whirling, and I don't know what happened or how my parents ended up with me. A kidnapped baby. I don't know why my mother had the baby bag and birth certificate in her closet or how it came to be there because I'd never seen it before that day. I don't know a lot of things, but I'm ready to find some answers."

He reached over to clasp her hand in his. Her strength and determination only made him admire her more. "You're a pretty amazing woman, you know that?"

She let out a low, humorless laugh. "No, I'm clinging to God with everything I have in me when all I really want to do is go home, bury my head under the covers and pretend this is all a bad dream." Tears floated to the surface again. And again she held them back. She lasered him with an intense look that shot straight to his heart. "I'm so glad I have you working on this with me, though. I really don't know what I would do without you," she whispered.

Her words rocked him, but didn't stop him from pulling her into a hug. "We'll get through this. I'm not going anywhere until you're safe and we have the answers you need."

"What if I never find them, Brandon? What if we just keep going in circles?"

He laid a light kiss on her lips, his desire to comfort her so strong it nearly strangled him. "Well, if you never find the answers, I guess that means I'm going to be around an awfully long time."

She flushed and he swiped a stray tear. "Thanks," she whispered.

"Welcome," he whispered back. Then let her go to start the car.

The twenty-minute drive to Don Bradley's office passed in a comfortable silence, both of them lost in their thoughts even though Brandon continued to keep an eye on their surroundings, alert for any hint of danger. But while his eyes roamed, his brain spun with his feelings for the lady beside him. She'd wiggled her way into his heart when he hadn't been looking. And that scared him. He hated to admit being afraid, especially since not much scared him.

His feelings for Sonya had him tied in knots. So what was he going to do about it?

Nothing.

She was a client.

Then you'd better stop kissing her. The thought taunted him. There was no way he wanted to lead her on, but the thought of her walking out of his life when all of this was over was simply unbearable.

He glanced at her. She had her eyes closed and her head against the window. Probably praying.

Maybe he should try it.

God? You know I believe in You even though I've been mad at You for a while now. Is it too late to ask for Your help? Not necessarily for me, but for Sonya. She really needs You. She believes You're there for her. She's hanging on to You. Could You just keep us safe? And help us figure out who wants us dead?

The prayer felt strange. And familiar.

He felt her gaze on him. "What are you thinking?" she asked.

"Nothing."

"Liar." The word lacked heat. It was a gentle rebuke that made him shoot her a rueful grin.

"Yeah. I wasn't really thinking. I was…praying."

That got her attention. Her brows shot up. "Really?"

"Yes."

"I didn't know you prayed."

He snorted. "I pray. Just not very often."

"Oh."

"I've been…mad at God. About a lot of stuff."

"Like your mom?"

He sighed. "Yes. Like my mom. And even my dad. But mostly my mom."

"Will you tell me why?"

He glanced at her again. The compassion in her eyes twisted his heart inside out. How could she do that to him with just one look? "I didn't have a horrible childhood, if that's what you're thinking."

"Oh. Well, yes, that's kind of what I was thinking."

"My parents were teenage sweethearts. They

got pregnant when my mother was sixteen. Instead of having parents raise us, we were all more or less like siblings. In the early part of our lives, my parents pretty much just ignored us. They partied. We were in the foster-care system a few times. Then they got us back after they took parenting classes and promised to party less." He narrated the story as though telling about someone else's life. It was the only way he could talk about it without the bitterness rising up to choke him. He looked at her. Felt her hand rest against his upper arm. He shrugged. "They started studying and going to school. Once we were old enough to be latchkey kids, we were. Mom became a nurse, Dad a mechanic. They worked all the time and we three kids fended for ourselves."

"But you turned out all right."

"We did. We had some good neighbors who kind of looked out for us. We even went to church with some of the other children in the neighborhood, catching a ride with whoever was going." He sighed. "It wasn't a miserable existence, but it wasn't ideal, either." He paused. "I wanted parents like some of the other kids had. The ones who came to the school plays and football games. I was quarterback and neither one of my parents ever made it to one of my games."

"Oh, Brandon, that's so sad."

"Exactly. And so now you know. I was angry

for a long time. Then I pushed it aside and focused on making something of my life."

"And what about your mother? She came to the station today."

"Yes. My mother." He shook his head. "She's trying to make up for lost time, I guess. She wants me to come to dinner Sunday."

"Are you going?"

"No." He heard the flat, cold word leave his lips. It effectively ended the conversation. That, and the fact that they'd arrived at their destination. He turned into the parking lot and found a spot under a shady tree.

He opened the door and stepped out of the car. His window exploded and he heard Sonya scream his name.

TWELVE

Sonya screamed again as the next bullet caught Brandon in his left shoulder. He went down. The few people in the parking lot took cover and grabbed for cell phones.

She scrambled across the seat to the open driver's door and grasped his hand to help pull him back into the ca-r. He slammed the door, his fingers searching for the seat button to push it back as far as it would go.

"Are you all right?" she gasped, terror pumping the blood through her veins in double time. "Let me look at it."

"It's a scratch. Call 911."

Sonya saw that his color was only a couple of shades lighter than normal and his shoulder wasn't bleeding much. She found her phone and punched in the three digits.

"911, what's your emergency?"

"Someone's shooting at us." She gave the address, wondering if the woman could understand her shaky words.

"Units are on the way. Stay in a safe area if at all possible."

Another shot took out the back window.

Brandon muttered something under his breath but Sonya didn't catch it. He lifted his head and stared out the back. "I see him. Stay here."

"What?"

But he didn't answer. He shoved the driver's door open and bolted toward the large industrial-sized trash can for cover. A bullet dinged off the metal. Sonya debated whether to run after Brandon, go for the building or stay put.

He made it to the next building and used one of the concrete columns in front as a shield. Another bullet. And another.

And then he was across the street.

Sonya opened her door and waited.

No bullets came her way.

She looked out the back window and saw a figure on the second floor of the parking garage across the street lift his gun, turn and run.

Sirens sounded. She made the final decision not to let Brandon face the would-be killer alone.

She bolted from the car and followed in his footsteps.

* * *

Brandon had seen the man with the gun on the second floor of the parking garage. This time he wasn't getting away. Ignoring the throbbing of the wound in his shoulder, he raced into the garage, his weapon held in both hands, pointing down.

Footsteps sounded above him. He raced toward them. A woman with a baby started to get out of her car. Brandon used his left hand to flash his badge. "Get back in the car and lock the door, then get out of the garage."

She gaped at the badge and the gun, then obeyed without question, her face pale and scared. He heard her start the car. He waited until she was headed for the exit before moving to the ramp that would take him to the second floor.

Brandon could hear the sirens. He needed to call in his location and request backup, but he didn't dare stop yet. He came to the end of the ramp.

Stopped and listened.

Nothing. No more footsteps. His heart thundered in his chest and his adrenaline flowed, but he kept his breathing even, his focus on the sounds and even smells around him.

From the second floor, he heard the sound of a car cranking. The shooter? Or another innocent person getting ready to ride into the path of danger?

Pulling in a deep breath, Brandon rounded the corner, weapon ready. Tires squealed on the concrete and a black Honda headed for him. Brandon caught sight of the masked face behind the wheel. He aimed his weapon and fired at the front left tire.

The rubber exploded and the car spun.

Running feet sounded behind him and he whirled to find other officers on the scene. He flashed his badge and turned back to the car.

And the now escaping suspect. "Freeze! Police!" The man never stopped. Brandon raced to the edge of the garage and looked over. "Cut him off! Cut him off!" The shooter ignored the stairwell and went for the ramp on the other end of the garage. "He's coming your way on the ramp!" he yelled to the officer below him. The officer responded by changing his direction and heading for the ramp. Brandon gave chase. The officers behind him followed.

Cruisers were now on the ground level. And still the fugitive managed to elude capture. He disappeared into the thick forest of trees that led to the Goethe River. A wild rushing mass of water, thanks to the waterfall not too far away.

On a hunch, Brandon headed for the bridge. He snagged his cell phone with his left hand and called in his position and where he was headed. Backup would follow. His footsteps pounded, his wound throbbed and his breaths came in fast pants, mostly from the pain, some from the extended running. He was in good shape, but he figured he was pushing somewhere near six miles.

Where was this guy? *Who* was this guy who could run this far and this long without stopping? Brandon kept his phone on and shoved it in his pocket. He had his Bluetooth in his ear and gave breathless updates every few seconds. A helicopter thumped above him. "Let me talk to the chopper." Dispatch patched him through. "Where is he?"

"To your left. Keep going. He's almost to the bridge. Cruisers are headed that way. One will stop on either side and trap him on the bridge."

"What about the people on it?"

"There are two pedestrians."

Brandon put on an extra burst of speed. He had to get to the bridge and get those people off before the suspect realized he was trapped. Brandon knew the man had left the rifle in the vehicle he'd abandoned, but he didn't know if he had another weapon or not.

Brandon arrived at the bridge seconds after the fleeing man. The two pedestrians, who looked to be in their mid-twenties, stood still, watching the masked man before horror and realization hit them. Then the young man grabbed the girl's hand. "Run!"

They took off. The first cruiser screeched to

a halt at the end of the bridge. The young couple scooted around it and dropped out of sight. The masked man stopped and spun. Saw Brandon and the cruiser blocking the way he'd just come. Brandon held his gun on him. "On the ground! Now!"

There weren't any weapons in sight, but that didn't mean he didn't have any. Brandon walked toward him. "You're trapped, dude. Give it up."

He didn't answer. Just backed toward the railing. Brandon approached with slow, even footsteps, keeping his weapon steady, ready for anything.

Sweat pooled at the small of his back and dripped from his face. He could only imagine how hot the mask was. The man's frantic eyes bounced from Brandon to the police officers who now approached, weapons drawn. "Come on," Brandon said. "You haven't hurt anyone yet. There's still a chance you could get off light."

"No way." He gripped the railing and Brandon realized what he planned. He lunged for him just as the man vaulted over the rail. Brandon reached the spot the shooter had just vacated and gripped the metal. He looked over in time to see the man hit the water hard and go under. Officers raced toward their vehicles, radios in hand, reporting the situation.

The chopper veered off and he knew they would do their best to see where the man surfaced. Brandon placed his hands on his knees then winced as his shoulder reminded him of the rough treatment it had recently received.

"Brandon?"

He turned to find Sonya climbing out of another police cruiser. He walked toward her. "Hey, what are you doing here?"

"I couldn't stay in the car. I saw the man leave the parking garage. I hitched a ride with this officer, who was willing to help me once I explained that I was in the car the guy was shooting at." She paused and bit her lip. "I saw him jump."

"Yeah."

"You think he'll be all right?" The doubt in her eyes told him what *she* thought.

Brandon shook his head. "I don't know, but he'll have to surface at some point, and when he does, we'll grab him."

"The police are everywhere. Surely he won't get away this time."

"Let's hope not." He took her hand and turned her toward the car.

She gasped when she saw his shoulder. "Your shoulder. It's more than a scratch."

He looked at the wound. "It's bled more because I've been moving."

"Will you let me look at it?"

The officer who'd given her the ride spoke for the first time. "We have EMTs on standby. Hop in and I'll take you to one."

"Great." She gave Brandon a gentle shove toward the police car. He hesitated with one more look toward the rushing river, then shook his head and gave in.

Sonya paced in the waiting room while Brandon was in the back getting patched up. Two officers stood guard over her at his insistence. As she paced, she touched the still-healing wound on her throat and thought.

She was missing something. Who would benefit from her death? The person who didn't want Heather Bradley found, obviously.

But why would someone not want the child found? What did it matter at this point if she was found or not? The only reason she could come up with was the adopted son. He didn't want her found because he felt threatened. But he had an alibi for the shooting. Then again, he could have hired someone.

"Sonya?"

She turned to find Don Bradley—her biological father—standing in the doorway. The officers moved closer. She nodded that it was all right and walked toward the man. "Hi."

"Is the detective all right?"

"He'll be fine. And I'm sure he wouldn't mind if you called him Brandon."

He gave a relieved smile. "I heard the shots

and saw all the craziness from my office window. Then I saw Brandon take off after him—" He swallowed hard and shook his head. "I'm so sorry this is happening. I don't understand why someone wouldn't want Heather found."

"We don't, either."

He motioned for her to sit and she did. He eased into the chair beside her, then looked her in the eye. "You're Heather, aren't you? That's what you were coming to tell me, isn't it?"

Sonya swallowed hard and gave a slow nod. "The DNA from the hair you supplied was a match. A hundred percent match."

"I see. You know, my wife's sister died shortly after you were born." His eyes shifted to the wall and she could tell his mind had gone to the past. "Those were hard days." His eyes reddened, but no tears appeared. "But we had you. You were the shining spot in my life." He reached over to grip her hand and Sonya let him. "I loved you with every fiber of my being—and then you were gone. And I felt I'd lost everything."

"I'm so sorry," she whispered.

He sniffed and blew out a breath, then stood and shoved his hands into his pockets.

Brandon appeared in the doorway and she rushed to him. "Are you okay?"

"Yes." He smiled and touched her cheek. "I'm

fine. A scratch like I said." He saw Don and held out a hand. "Guess you heard the commotion."

"And then some." Don shook his hand. "Sonya just told me the news."

Brandon nodded. "I hated to tell you over the phone."

The man gave him a small smile. "When you didn't say it, I knew."

"I figured you probably did."

A woman entered the waiting room. Sonya recognized Brandon's sister, Erica. Brandon spotted her at the same time. Erica made a beeline for her brother. "Shot? Really? Again?"

Brandon hugged and shushed her. "Stop. It's barely there. Only needed five stitches and some antibiotics. Already had the tetanus up to date and I'm good to go. Won't even need physical therapy."

Erica looked as if she was ready to add to her brother's pain. "Are you insane?"

He sighed. "Not last I checked. I'm fine, Erica."

"Where was Max or Peter or Jordan or Frankie? Or *someone*?"

His jaw tightened. "They can't babysit twenty-four-seven."

"Of course they can," she snapped. Sonya watched the two siblings snipe at each other a moment longer before Erica's shoulders drooped. "You just scared me."

Brandon softened at his sister's sincere worry.

He wrapped his good arm around her. "I know. I'm sorry. I'll be more careful."

It was her turn to sigh. "No, you won't." She pulled away.

Sonya exchanged a glance with Don. He shook his head, a small smile playing on his lips in spite of the seriousness of the situation. Sonya felt a pang in the vicinity of her heart. Growing up, she'd always wanted a brother or sister, and now watching Erica and Brandon, she realized she still did.

"What's your son's name?" she asked Don.

"Grayson."

"How will he feel when he learns about me?"

"Thrilled. He grew up knowing he had a sister. He's always said he wished she—you—would turn up one day."

Sonya nodded. "Maybe soon we could meet. After the craziness is over. I don't want to put him in danger."

"Of course." He shook his head. "He used to pretend his nanny was his sister, but after we lost Heather—you—having another girl just seemed… wrong somehow." He flushed. "Silly, I know."

"Nanny?" Brandon asked.

Don blinked. "Er…yes." He gave a little laugh. "My wife loves being a mother, but she also loves her social life." His lips twisted in a sad smile. "It was just easier to hire live-in help. With time off, of course."

"Of course."

Sonya knew exactly what was clicking through Brandon's mind. "Did I have a nanny?" she asked.

His brows lifted. "Um…well…yes, as a matter of fact, you did."

"Was she the same nanny Grayson had?"

"No. I called to check on her one time and found she'd moved."

"Moved where?"

"I'm not sure. No one said."

"What's her name?"

"Rebecca Gold."

"You think she would talk to us?"

Don frowned. "Why?"

"She was Heather's nanny. I want to ask her if she saw anything suspicious the day Heather was taken."

"But she wasn't at church that morning."

"Are you sure?"

"Of course I'm sure. She didn't even go to that church." He paused. "You're not thinking she took Heather, are you?"

"The possibility crossed my mind," Brandon said.

"But the police talked to her and cleared her."

"Maybe they just didn't ask the right questions."

THIRTEEN

Brandon's phone rang. Hector's number winked up at him. "Hello?"

"Are you all right? Heard you got nicked."

"I'm fine. And yes, thankfully, a nick is all it was."

"Your lady friend all right?"

Brandon glanced at Sonya, who appeared deep in conversation with Don Bradley. Her father. "She's hanging in there."

"You like her, don't you?"

Brandon snorted. "Do I *like* her? Are we back in high school now?"

"Fess up, partner."

Brandon turned serious. "Yes. I like her."

His simple statement seemed to throw Hector for a loop. Silence echoed back at him. Then Hector cleared his throat. "Well. Good. I…uh… Well, that's nice, Brandon. I'm happy for you."

Brandon smiled. He'd finally said something to

make his partner go speechless. That was one for the books. "Keep me updated."

"Yeah. Yeah. And you learn how to duck a little faster, huh?"

"I'll see what I can do."

Brandon hung up and grimaced. His shoulder throbbed. Thankfully, it was the same side he'd taken a bullet in about a year ago. At least he still had one good arm. And this bullet hadn't even penetrated, just skimmed the surface. Still stung, though.

He walked over to Sonya. "Are you ready to go?"

"I guess so. The question is—are you?"

"I'm ready." He looked at Don. "I'm sorry for all the chaos looking into Heather's disappearance is causing. I hope this doesn't come back on you. What's your home security system like?"

The man shook his head. "My security system is state-of-the-art. After we adopted Grayson, Ann insisted. And I'm simply stunned with everything that's happened. It just doesn't make sense."

"It makes sense to whoever is trying to stop us." Brandon pulled the keys from his pocket. "I'm going to take Sonya home and get a little rest myself. We'll regroup and figure out a plan where to go from here."

"I want to talk to the nanny," Sonya said.

"I've got Hector tracking her down. As soon as we have an address, we'll pay her a visit."

Don stepped forward and took Sonya's hand. "I want to get to know you."

Brandon saw Sonya swallow hard. "I want that, too," she said, "but I don't think someone else is too excited about the idea."

"I don't care. We'll fight back together."

"No. I don't want to put you in danger. After this is over, we'll talk, okay?"

He looked at Brandon. "I want to help."

Brandon frowned. "I understand that, sir, but I don't really know what you can do at this point."

"What if Sonya comes to stay with us? My wife and I would love to have her. And I just told you we have a state-of-the-art security system."

"Oh, I don't know about that," Sonya said. "I'd have to think about it." She bit her lip and backed up a fraction.

Brandon wondered what was going through her mind. Sheer panic blossomed and she shot him a desperate look. He stepped over and put his arm around her. "We'll talk about it," he said. "It's actually not a bad idea, but give us some time to discuss it."

"Of course." The man shoved his hands into his pockets. "I didn't mean to push too hard."

"No, it's okay," Sonya said. She'd gathered herself together quickly and Brandon wanted to think his presence helped her do so. "Like Brandon said, I'll…think about it."

Don nodded and took a step toward the door. "I'll leave now." He shot a beseeching look at Sonya. "But please do think about it. I've lost almost twenty-eight years with you. I guess I just don't want to lose another minute."

Sonya said nothing more. She simply nodded.

He patted the front pocket of his blazer, then reached in and pulled out a small packet. "Before I forget. These are some pictures of our family. I thought you might like to see them."

Sonya took them. "Thank you. I definitely would like to look at them." She slipped them into her purse.

Don left.

Brandon turned to Sonya. "You don't have to stay with them, don't worry."

She gave a small shrug. "If I thought Mrs. Bradley wanted me to, I might consider it, but I'd never invade her home like that knowing how she feels about me."

Erica, who'd been standing by, observing and listening, turned to Brandon. "We've got resources, you know. If you need a safe house, it could probably be arranged."

Sonya shook her head. "No. No safe house." She pulled in a deep breath. "If I go into hiding, I'll never be able to come out." Her lips firmed and her chin jutted. "I'm going to stay in plain sight and just pray we catch him before he catches me."

Sonya wanted to recall her pseudobrave words. The harsh frown on Brandon's face said he didn't like them, either. But she couldn't take the words back and decided then she didn't want to. She knew if she disappeared, she'd never be able to have a real life again. Not as herself, anyway. She couldn't live like that. She had to find the truth and find it soon. She prayed that the Lord saw fit to let her live to do it.

Brandon escorted her from the hospital. She thought he looked pale and drawn. His shoulder had to be hurting him.

They stepped outside and Brandon came to an abrupt halt. "I don't have a car."

"No, but I do." Erica, who'd been following silently behind, smiled sweetly and swung her keys at them.

Brandon smiled. "Right. So is Max pulling protection duty tonight?"

Max, Erica's husband, didn't mind helping out when needed. And he was definitely needed tonight.

"Max and Peter." Erica led the way to her vehicle.

Sonya scanned the area. Was he watching? Was he wondering how they'd once again managed to elude him? Or had he drowned in the river? Was it all over?

They arrived at Erica's dark blue SUV, and Sonya saw Max parked next to Erica.

He rolled the window down as they approached. "Ready to roll?"

Brandon shook his hand. "What are you doing here?"

"Erica's the chauffeur. I'm the escort."

Sonya relaxed a fraction.

"I've also asked Jordan to be at the house when you're home tonight. You need to be able to rest without worrying about an intruder," Max said.

Jordan Gray. Sonya recognized the name. She hadn't met the other agency operative, but knew he was Brandon's roommate. The one who was marrying Katie Randall, a detective Brandon had worked with on occasion. When she'd first approached Finding the Lost, he'd given her the rundown on all of the employees.

Brandon motioned for Sonya to take the front passenger seat then opened the door. He looked at Max with a frown. "That's not necessary."

"Well, I think it is." Erica lifted her chin a notch and gave her brother a steely-eyed look. "And Jordan agreed with us. He'll be there when I drop you off. Peter is on the way to Missy's as we speak."

"And I'll be joining him shortly," Max said. Sonya listened to them go back and forth and leaned her head back against the headrest. It was all just too much. *I don't understand why this is happening, Lord, but don't let my faith waver now. When Dad died, I was devastated. When my mom died, I was ready to crumble. I begged You for peace, but didn't get it. I still don't know that I've truly accepted she's gone. That they're both gone. Please help me, Lord.*

The plea seemed to bring a measure of comfort. She didn't know if that was the Lord or if she just felt better after getting it off her chest. But she'd asked God for peace and now she felt better. She wasn't going to take that away from Him. *Thank You, Lord.*

Exhaustion swamped her.

Brandon's phone rang and she turned her attention to his conversation. "Who? Right. Okay, I'll ask him. Thanks."

"Who was that?" Erica asked before Sonya could get the words out.

"Hector."

"What did he want?"

"He's been investigating the Bradleys."

"And?" Sonya perked up.

"He said they came back clean. Squeaky-clean. No record of any kind."

"Oh, well, that's good, right?"

"Yes, it's great. He did mention that Mrs. Bradley's sister died shortly after Heather was born."

"Mr. Bradley mentioned that," Sonya said.

"Did he mention how she died?"

"No, just that it was a really hard time in his family. Heather was kidnapped—" Sonya simply couldn't refer to herself as Heather "—and his sister-in-law died."

"Apparently she fell down a flight of stairs and broke her neck."

Sonya gasped. "How awful!"

"Mrs. Bradley said she'd been depressed and had talked of killing herself, so they briefly wondered if it was suicide, but in the end it was ruled an accident."

"Suicide by throwing yourself down a flight of stairs?" Sonya scoffed. "That doesn't even make sense. Who does that?"

Erica pulled into Missy's drive and Brandon nodded. "I thought the same thing, but apparently there was no evidence of foul play."

"So it was just a tragic accident."

"Looks like."

Brandon's phone rang before he could climb out of the car. "Hello?"

"Me again," Hector trilled in a falsetto pitch.

"That's so annoying."

"I know. That's why I do it," Hector said in his normal voice. "I'll get right to it. We found your jumper or the shooter—whichever label you want to put on him."

"The guy I chased from the parking garage."

"Yep. He washed downstream and our guys pulled him out."

"Anything else?"

"Yeah. He left his weapon in the car. We're running ballistics on it even as we speak."

Even though Brandon and Hector both knew without a shadow of a doubt the guy was guilty, they needed hard evidence. Linking the gun and the bullets to him would prove he was the shooter.

"Have them check it against the one used in the park shooting," Brandon said.

Silence echoed back at him, and then Hector said, "Excellent idea. I'll have them do that as soon as we get off the phone."

"That's twice Sonya's been shot at. It wouldn't surprise me a bit if the bullets came from the same gun."

"But what about the other two women who were shot?"

"I don't know what the connection is. Why don't you do a little investigating on that, too?"

"All right. I'll see if Sonya has any link with those two and I'll call ballistics as soon as we hang up. What else?"

"Any information on Rebecca Gold?"

"Nothing yet. Still looking."

"Okay. Let's get back to the shooter, then."

"Right. Well, he's dead."

Brandon rolled his eyes. "I figured that. That was a pretty long drop off the bridge."

"Yeah. And the water's not more than four feet deep."

"Did he drown?"

"Broke his neck along with some other bones, but the neck injury killed him. He's definitely our guy from the photograph, though. The tattoo on his shoulder matches the one in the picture."

Brandon blew out a sigh. "Okay, what's his name? Did he have any ID on him?"

"No ID on him, but we ran his prints and he's in the system. Name's Buddy Reed."

"Should I know him?"

"No reason to. But he has a record. Armed robbery is his biggest offense when he was eighteen. It was a one-time deal and he got a slap on the wrist since no one was hurt. He seemed to get his act together and got his degree in sports medicine. Right now, he's a trainer at one of the local gyms. Or, rather, he was."

"Any experience with guns? Weapons?"

"Well, since he missed hitting you, I'm guessing not much. Then again, he had pretty good aim in the park if he's the same shooter." Hector paused and Brandon heard the rustling of papers. "But no, there's nothing other than the armed robbery. No

military service, no guns registered in his name.
I'm guessing the rifle he had was off the black
market. The serial number was filed off. I'll keep
looking into everything."

"Good. That would be great."

"You sound distracted."

Brandon blinked. "I'm just wondering if it's
over."

"What do you mean? The shooter's dead. The
danger's over, right?"

"Unless he was working for someone, and that
someone just hires another killer when he learns
of Buddy Reed's demise." Of course that was a
possibility. "We'll keep the protection-detail plans
for tonight and revisit it in the morning. Thanks
for the info."

"My pleasure. See ya."

Click.

Brandon hung up the phone and turned to
Sonya. She'd heard every word. "He's dead?"

"Yes."

"So is it over? I can go home?"

"Hector and I discussed the possibility that the
guy could have been working for someone."

She blanched. "Oh."

"So, let's keep up the precautions and see where
we are in the morning." The same thing he'd said
to Hector.

She nodded. "Fine." But she couldn't help feeling massive amounts of relief. The man who'd shot at her was dead. She could sleep tonight. Maybe. If it hadn't been someone who'd been hired. If that was the case, then both she and Brandon were still in danger.

FOURTEEN

Thankfully, the night passed without incident. Brandon woke to find his phone had no missed calls. His shoulder throbbed but wasn't painful enough to keep him down. In the bathroom, he popped three Advil tablets, showered, shaved and decided he was ready to face the day.

After a cup of coffee—or three.

In the kitchen, he found Jordan sitting at the table reading the morning paper on his iPad. "You get any sleep last night?" Brandon asked him.

"A little."

"You didn't have to play bodyguard, you know."

"I know, but you slept better knowing I was doing it, didn't you?"

Brandon let out a short laugh. "Yeah, actually I did."

"Then it was worth it. How's the shoulder this morning?"

"Sore."

"You need me for anything today?"

Brandon shook his head. "No." He glanced at his phone. "I'm waiting for Hector to get back to me on a few things. I need to know where Ms. Gold is and I want to know about the ballistics report. Once I have those two things, I'll be able to plan the next course of action." He poured himself a cup of coffee and added cream and sugar. "Other than that, I plan to send Max and Peter home and spend the day with Sonya, making sure she's safe." He took his first sip of the brew and closed his eyes with pleasure. Three more sips and he felt himself start to wake up.

"You don't think it's over."

Brandon looked at his roommate and lifted a brow. "Do you?"

Jordan shrugged. "I don't know. But I think you're doing the right thing."

"What's that?"

"Staying on guard, until you know for sure."

He nodded and slipped into the chair opposite Jordan. "Do you mind if I ask you something?"

"Of course not. You've never asked permission before."

Brandon smirked. "Right." He sighed. "How'd you know Katie was the one?"

"Ahhhh…"

"What's that mean?"

"Sonya."

Brandon flushed. "Yeah."

Instead of teasing him like he thought he would, Jordan turned thoughtful. "You know, when we first met, she was looking for Molly. Erica was a basket case and I wasn't exactly in a good frame of mind. But last year—" he shook his head "—when Katie was in all that danger because she was looking for her sister and we were working together, something just sparked, you know?" He lifted a shoulder. "She was spunky and determined and— hurting. But she was a fighter and I really liked that about her. Like eventually turned to love."

"She and Sonya sound a lot alike."

Jordan nodded. "Then she's a keeper."

"It's looking like it."

"But?"

"But you know my history. And you know about Krystal. How do I know Sonya will be able to deal with my baggage? My family?"

"You don't. Until you trust her with it."

"Right. Easier said than done."

Jordan hesitated. "You know, it's not my place to lecture you, but your parents are trying to do the right thing. If you'd let go of all that anger, there's still time to build a relationship with them."

Tension immediately filled Brandon. "You sound like Peter."

"Sounds like Peter's getting some smarts." Jordan shut off the iPad and stood. "On that note, I'm going to go into the office."

"And I'm going to head over to Missy's."

"You want me to follow you?"

Brandon paused. "It's on the way, so why not? Keep an eye on my tail and see if you spot anything."

"Will do."

Brandon arrived at Missy's house with no tail in sight. As Jordan pulled away with a wave, Brandon wondered if he'd crossed the line onto the paranoia side. Max gave him a salute and left. Brandon knew he and Erica were having breakfast together. Peter lingered at the curb, so Brandon walked over to speak to his brother. He had the window down and was sipping on coffee he'd brought in a thermos. "How's it going?"

"It's been quiet." He lifted the thermos top posing as a cup. "Good thing I had this stuff or I would have been snoozing."

"But you didn't snooze, right?"

Peter's face darkened. "Of course not. You gave me a job to do and I'm doing it."

Brandon let his gaze linger on his younger brother's face. "Yeah. You are. And you're doing a good job, too. Thanks."

The darkness cleared and Peter swallowed. "It's the least I can do. You're giving me a second chance." He snorted. "Or maybe it's a third, fourth or fifth chance. I don't know. I've lost count at this point, I guess."

"I'm not keeping track. You're putting your life back together. That's all that matters."

"Are you coming to Mom and Dad's for dinner Sunday night?"

Brandon straightened and, at the mention of his parents, felt the familiar squeeze in the vicinity of his temple. "No."

"Why not?"

"You know why not." He kept his words low and even, not letting them explode like he wanted to.

Peter snorted. "They're trying, Brandon. They were young and on their own and didn't know what they were doing. Can't you find a way to forgive and move on?"

For a second, he almost relented. But the bad memories crowded out the moment. "I…I…can't. It's too late."

Peter sighed. "Don't you want a relationship with them?"

Brandon flinched. "No. Not really." As soon as the words left his lips, he realized they were a lie. He did want a relationship with his parents. He just didn't know how to get over the past. How did he let go of all the disappointment and hurt that had been such a part of his life? The pain that had shaped him into part of who he was today? He shook his head. "No, I'm not ready for that. Not yet."

"Will you ever be ready?"

"That's a question I can't answer right now."

"You know, in rehab we talked a lot about forgiveness—forgiving ourselves and asking forgiveness of others. Been going to church, too, and listening to sermons on the topic. It's been pretty eye-opening."

Brandon took a step back and planted his hands on his hips. He opened his mouth, but Peter lifted a hand to cut him off. "I'm not giving you a speech, just saying bitterness and an unforgiving heart can be as destructive as cocaine or meth. I may be the recovering addict, but you're the one who needs some rehab. Some heart rehab. Think about it." He cranked the car and drove off without another word.

Brandon let his brother's words rattle around in his brain for the next ten seconds. Then he turned to find Sonya standing behind him, face bright red, looking awkward and uncomfortable. She sighed. "I'm sorry. I didn't mean to interrupt. Or eavesdrop."

"It's a long-standing argument. Don't worry about it." He managed to get the words through his clenched teeth.

She chewed her bottom lip for a moment and he waited for the question. "Is he right?"

"No." His conscience shouted *liar,* but he ignored it.

"Hmm. Okay."

He motioned to his car. "Come on. I don't want you standing out here in the open."

"The shooter's dead, remember?"

"Right, but until we know for sure that this is over, I want you inside."

"Okay." She sighed and turned to go back into the house. He followed her, head swiveling left then right. He saw nothing that alarmed him, but wasn't dropping his guard. "Want to grab some breakfast?"

She eyed him and shrugged. "Sure. Are you feeling okay?"

"Food will take my mind off the aggravation."

"All right, then. Just let me get my purse."

"Hey, bring those pictures Don gave you, okay? I want to look over them."

"Sure." She disappeared inside.

Brandon's internal struggle didn't cease just because Peter had left and Sonya's all-seeing eyes were no longer on him. He stepped onto the porch and sat in one of the white wicker rockers. He let his gaze roam the street, probing into the shadows, watching for anything that looked as if it shouldn't belong. Even as he stayed alert and focused on his surroundings, Peter's words continued to ring in his mind. *Bitterness and an unforgiving heart can be as destructive as cocaine or meth.*

On an intellectual level, Brandon knew his brother was right. On an emotional one, he wanted to deny it. He remembered after Peter came home from rehab, one of the first things he'd done was ask his family for forgiveness. And Brandon had granted it without reservation.

He wasn't bitter or unforgiving; he was apathetic. Toward his parents, anyway. They hadn't needed him when he was younger, hadn't been supportive or even very caring. They'd been indifferent—and selfish. More focused on having a good time and partying than they'd been on raising kids.

It wasn't that he was even still angry with them. Was he? Brandon snorted. Yes, he was. He was angry, but he didn't need them. Or their sudden desire to be involved in his and his siblings' lives.

He flashed back to a day at the park. He'd been about eight years old. They'd had a family picnic, and he recalled laughter and his father pushing him on a swing, high-fiving him after his descent down the slide.

Brandon blinked. Where had that come from? Had he made it up? No. He remembered the park. He frowned. Were there other good memories he'd suppressed in his determination to hold on to his anger?

"I'm ready."

Her soft voice pulled Brandon from his thoughts. Casually dressed in a pink tank top and khaki capris, he thought she looked beautiful. Even the stitches covered by a small Band-Aid at the base of her throat didn't detract from her loveliness.

He rose and took her elbow to help guide her down the steps and over to his car. Warmth radiated from her and he swallowed. She was warm and compassionate, caring and generous. Everything his ex-fiancée had appeared to be on the surface. She'd enjoyed the status dating him had given her among her friends. Dating a police detective had been a big deal to her.

Until she'd gotten tired of the long hours. And the fact that he didn't make enough to support her in the lifestyle she wanted.

He wondered if Sonya would be able to handle it. As a nurse, she understood long hours and hard work. The irony of her profession hadn't escaped him. A nurse. Just like his mother. And yet, the two women seemed vastly different. He just couldn't picture his mother as compassionate.

Then again, he hadn't really been around her that much lately to make that judgment.

But he didn't think he could possibly be wrong.

Sonya wondered if Brandon could possibly be wrong. Wrong about it not being over. Ever since the shooter's death, things had been quiet.

Ominously quiet?

Maybe. She shivered.

He drove with precision. She watched him

navigate the roads, clearly thinking deeply about something, yet attentive and aware of their surroundings.

He glanced at her and caught her watching. She flushed and looked away.

"Why did you become a nurse, almost a doctor?" he asked.

She blinked at the random question. "Because I care about people, about helping them." She shrugged. "And I like science and medicine. The human body is a fascinating, intricately designed machine. That intrigues me."

"Do you plan to go back to school and finish the classes you need to become a doctor?"

"Yes. As soon as I can." Sadness engulfed her. "My mother would want that. She felt so bad that I had to quit school to come back and take care of her."

"Did she have any brothers or sisters?"

"No, both she and my dad were only children."

Brandon pulled into the parking lot of one of the downtown cafés. As they walked into the building, he placed a hand at the small of her back to guide her. She shivered, feeling the warmth of his touch. First her elbow, then her back. He was comfortable enough with her to offer the simple touches. Innocent gestures that spoke of a growing closeness.

And she was comfortable enough to accept the

touches—and the growing closeness. If only he could resolve his issues with his family. But he said he didn't date clients. Which was something she could understand. Didn't mean she liked it, but she could respect it.

She had a feeling he didn't like it so much himself. A small smile pulled at her lips at the thought. "You like this place."

He nodded. "I like their coffee. And just about everything else they serve here."

"Are you really still concerned that someone is still after me?"

"Not as concerned as I was before we found out the shooter was dead."

"But?"

"But I don't think it hurts to stay cautious until we know for sure."

Once they'd ordered, picked up their food and settled into a booth—facing the door, she noticed—Sonya said, "Do you mind if I bless it?"

He shifted, but didn't seem uneasy. He nodded and she bowed her head. "Thank You, Lord, for this food. For Your protection. Please let this thing be over. And thank You for putting Brandon in my life at just the right time."

When she lifted her head she found his eyes on her, warm and smoky. "That was a nice prayer."

Embarrassed, she shrugged. "That was a really nice thing you did for Spike and his mother."

"Spike's a good kid. He got into a lot of trouble two years ago, was hooked on meth and any other kind of drug he could get his hands on. I busted him during a drug sting."

"And now he thinks you hung the moon."

Brandon flushed and shrugged. "I gave him a chance."

"He reminded you of you—or what you could have been, didn't he?" she asked softly.

He jerked and took a sip of his coffee then a bite of his bagel. "Yes."

She nodded. "Why didn't you end up like Spike?"

He sighed. "I don't know." He tapped his fingers on the table, then seemed to make up his mind. "I mean, my parents weren't into criminal stuff—other than underage drinking—but I don't think they ever used drugs. At least none that I saw. They just weren't there. And while I was angry about it, I was still looking for something to connect with. That was sports. Football, basketball, anything to keep moving and not think too much. As much freedom as I had growing up, I knew if I got into drugs, I'd ruin my future."

"So you decided to make the right choices?"

"In a roundabout way. I wanted to play sports and couldn't do that if I was strung out or high. Once I got out of high school, I had a full ride to college on a football scholarship. I didn't want to

mess that up. Throw in Erica's preaching and seeing what drugs had done to Peter—" He shrugged.

"So that's why you're so involved in Parker
House. You want to give kids another alternative."

"Yes."

"You're a good, strong man, Brandon Hayes."

He flushed. "Thanks." Silence descended as
they ate. Then Brandon's phone buzzed and he
grabbed it. "Hector, just who I wanted to hear
from. What do you have?"

"I've got an address on your nanny."

"Great. Text it to me, will you?"

"Already done. I also found out she's working
as a nanny for another couple in Charlotte, North
Carolina. Tomorrow's her day off."

"How'd you find that out?"

"I have my ways."

Brandon grunted. "Thanks." He hung up and
looked at Sonya. "Feel like a road trip tomorrow?"

"Sure. Technically, I'm still on medical leave."

His gaze dropped to her throat. "How's it feeling?"

"Still sore, of course, but healing."

"Are you staying with Missy tonight?"

"Do you think I should?"

"Probably."

She gave a nod. "Then I will. Missy said I have
an open invitation. The one good thing about

this whole mess is that I think I'm making a life-long friend."

"Nothing like looking on the positive side of things."

She rolled her eyes. "Well, it's better than the alternative."

"Did you bring those pictures Don gave you?"

She pulled them from her purse and handed them to him. "Why don't you slide around here so we can look at them together," he said.

Her heart tumbled over itself in eager agreement to be that close to him. She got up and slid in the booth next to him. He radiated warmth. Security. She scooted closer until her arm brushed his. She looked up at him and found him staring at her. His eyes dropped to her lips. Then he swallowed and fanned the pictures on the table. He cleared his throat. "So. Ah. Look."

Sonya leaned forward to see the first one. Don and Ann Bradley stood on the front porch of their house. Don held Heather, and Ann stood with her hand on the baby's head. They looked happy. "That must have been when they brought me home from the hospital." She sighed. "It's like staring at strangers. I can't bring myself to even think of them as my parents."

They continued to flip through the pictures. Sonya stopped and pulled one out. "Look. Who's that?" A woman held her, but it wasn't Ann—her mother—no, Ann. Sonya firmed her jaw.

She had a mother, and while that mother was dead, she'd have a hard time calling another by the name. "She looks similar to Ann. I wonder if that's the sister who died."

"Is anything written on the back?"

She flipped it over. "'Miriam and Heather.'"

"Miriam. I don't know that Hector ever said her name." He frowned and picked up the phone. "I'll call Don and ask him." He dialed the man's number and Sonya went through the rest of the pictures. It appeared that Heather had a couple of cousins, each who took turns holding her. "A happy family," she whispered.

Brandon hung up and she jumped. She'd missed the conversation. "What did he say?"

"He said it was Miriam, Ann's sister who died."

"The one who fell down the steps," she murmured. "Did they say how that happened exactly?"

"No, Mrs. Bradley—Ann—went to check on her sister and found her at the bottom of the steps."

"That's awful. Poor Ann."

He nodded then went rigid, his hard gaze on something beyond her right shoulder. "Brandon? What is it?"

"My parents."

Sonya turned and saw two people in their midforties heading their way.

The woman had her bright red hair pulled back into a loose ponytail. The man had on an auto-mechanic uniform. Grease stains dotted the gray material.

"Brandon. I'm so glad we ran into you," the woman gushed.

Brandon gave a brief nod. "We were just leaving." He nudged Sonya, who stood. Brandon followed. Pain flashed in Shelby's eyes, but she did her best to cover it with a smile. "Won't you introduce us?"

After a brief hesitation, he placed a hand on Sonya's back. "Sonya, this is my mother, Shelby Hayes, and my father, Brant Hayes."

Sonya smiled and held out a hand to each of them. "So glad to meet you."

Shelby gave her fingers a light squeeze then turned to her son. "Brandon, we'd love to have you come Sunday for dinner. Erica and Peter will be there and we've invited Jordan and Katie, too. Won't you come?"

"Probably not. I'm working a case."

The hope in his mother's eyes faded to a deep sadness. Sonya felt her heart wrench for the woman. "Of course," Shelby said. "I understand."

"Well, I don't," his father growled. "You gonna punish us forever? You're so perfect you've never made a mistake?"

"Back off." Brandon's low warning sent shivers up Sonya's spine. "This isn't the place."

Brant shook his head. "Come on, Shelby. Give it up. He's never going to let go of his anger."

Brandon's mother sighed and tears filled her eyes. "Why was it so easy to forgive Peter all the lousy things he's done over the years, but you can't find it in your heart to accept a plea for forgiveness from your parents? Can't you just give us a chance to prove we've changed?"

Sonya's heart ached at the coldness in Brandon's gaze. Yet beneath the chill, she thought she saw a glimmer of longing. He didn't answer, just took Sonya's hand and pulled her from the restaurant.

Once outside and in the car he said, "All right, we have a game plan. I'm going to head back to my office and get some work done."

"Which office?"

"Finding the Lost. I've got a couple days off from the force."

"Okay. Then just drop me at Missy's. It'll be good to hang out with her for a while."

"Fine."

She wondered if he would say anything about his parents. His tight jaw and narrowed eyes said he was still thinking about the incident. After thirty seconds of silence he shook his head and looked at her. "I'm sorry about that."

"It's okay, Brandon."

"No, it's not."

"I'm wondering about the question your mother asked you."

"Which one?"

"About why it seemed to be so easy for you to forgive Peter, but you can't give them another chance."

He flexed his fingers on the wheel. "I don't know." His low, agony-filled answer made her heart ache anew for him.

"Your father is right. They're humans with faults just like all the rest of us. Keep trying to get past what happened when they were too young to be parents and focus on the fact that they want to right their wrongs."

He took a deep breath and she thought he might argue with her. He didn't. He simply stared out the window. Finally, he cleared his throat. "I'll pick you up in the morning?"

"That'll be fine." She let the subject go. If he wouldn't open up to her and let her help, he would have to work through the emotional baggage he carried by himself. She gripped his fingers. "I'm here if you need me, Brandon. I'll just be a non-judgmental listening ear if you need it."

He gave her hand an answering squeeze. "I'll be looking forward to tomorrow."

The thought of spending the whole day with him tomorrow sent shivers chasing one another all over her skin. She only hoped they didn't have to spend the day looking over their shoulders and dodging people who wanted them dead.

FIFTEEN

Thursday morning dawned hot and humid. Brandon picked Sonya up at eight o'clock sharp. He'd missed her after he'd dropped her off yesterday. Missed her a lot. He'd thought about her off and on all afternoon, her face appearing in his thoughts at odd moments even as he met with Erica and Jordan to discuss the other ongoing cases. He caught them up on Sonya and her case, then went home to rest. He hated to admit it, but his shoulder had been killing him.

Jordan followed him home and had spent the day playing bodyguard while Brandon grabbed some much-needed sleep. Max had taken the afternoon off to watch over Sonya and Missy.

Nothing happened during the night, and Brandon almost questioned whether he was just being paranoid in keeping such close tabs on Sonya now that the shooter was dead.

And yet, something niggled at him. He wasn't quite ready to believe that it was that easy. He felt in his gut that someone had hired that man to go after Sonya. And until that person was behind bars, Sonya was still in danger.

She stepped out onto the porch and he caught his breath. Which made him squirm. No woman had affected him like this. Not even his ex-fiancée.

She slid into the passenger seat and shot him a smile. "You've become quite adept at playing chauffeur over the past few days, haven't you?"

"I don't mind. I'm sorry it's necessary, but I don't mind." He ran a finger down her cheek. "Spending time with you is always the highlight of my day."

She shivered at his touch then blinked as though his straightforward bluntness had caught her off guard. He had to admit, it surprised him, too. "You're a very confusing man sometimes."

He felt his lips tilt higher. "Trust me, I'm not nearly as confusing as you."

"Why's that?"

"Because you're a woman. Women have the market on confusing."

She gaped at him. "I can't believe you said that. Are you stereotyping me?"

He swooped in and captured her lips with his for a brief moment. "Never," he whispered.

Her eyes locked on his. "Well. Good. I'm glad you cleared that up."

He leaned back. "But you're a client." Even as the words left his lips, he wanted to recall them.

"Yes. I am."

"And I don't get involved with clients."

She flushed and raised a brow, a tinge of anger darkening her already dark eyes. "Really? So you just kiss them."

He sighed and clasped her fingers in his. "No, I'm sorry. Not for kissing you," he clarified quickly. "But you're right. I'm—attracted to you, Sonya, and it's sending my heart spinning. Frankly, I'm not sure what to do about it."

She blinked. "Oh. The fact that you're laying this out here is really out of character for you, isn't it?" she murmured.

He gave a low laugh. "Tell me about it. But—" he ran a hand through his hair and sighed "—I know life is short, but these last few days of eluding death have really hit home. I want you to know that I *don't* go around kissing clients—or any woman, for that matter. I want you to know I'm not playing games with your heart."

"But you're going to table your feelings until all of this is resolved."

"Yes. I think I have to. I need to focus on making sure that you're safe."

She nodded. "Okay. If that's what you have to do."

"But when this is over—"

"I get it, Brandon."

He tilted her chin toward him. "I hope so. I really do." Then he let her go and pulled away from the curb.

Well, if Brandon's heart was spinning, Sonya decided hers was playing copycat. The man had her emotions all over the place. And yet, she appreciated his honesty.

She also had to admit she'd let her imagination swing toward shopping for white dresses and pretty flowers. Every once in a while and when she'd needed a distraction from the crazy danger. But he was right. This wasn't the time in their lives to be thinking about that. Worrying about staying alive should be priority.

But later, when all of this was over...

The drive to Rebecca Gold's house took a little over an hour with Brandon watching the mirrors the whole time.

She and Brandon made small talk the rest of the way, dancing around the topic of relationships and kissing. That was fine with her. She needed her emotions to settle down.

When he pulled into the drive, she took in the residence. A brick ranch house in a nice middle-class area with a beautifully manicured yard. A white Toyota Camry sat in the single carport.

"Did you call her and tell her we were coming?" Sonya asked.

"No. I didn't want to give her a heads-up. If she was involved in the kidnapping in any way, I was afraid she'd run."

"What makes you think she was actually involved?"

"I don't. Just speculation. But in thinking that it was someone close to the family, after the parents, she's the next logical suspect."

"I wondered if she might have been involved. For the same reasons." Sonya opened the door and climbed from the vehicle. She shivered in spite of the hot sun blazing down on her. She walked around to Brandon's side.

"Let's try the front door."

Sonya walked up the steps and knocked. Brandon stood at her back, turned away from her, watching the street. She knocked again.

Nothing.

"She's not here, I guess," Sonya said.

"Her car is in the carport."

"Maybe she's taking a walk."

"Maybe." He looked doubtful. "Let's go around to the back."

Sonya followed him around the side of the house. The grass was sod, making a smooth green path to the back. Carefully tended flowers bloomed along the edges, and she could clearly see someone enjoyed her yard work.

A small patio led to a back door. Brandon

started to knock, then paused. Sonya stepped closer. "What is it?"

"The door's open."

"And look at those flowers." She pointed to the other side of the porch. "They're crushed like someone stepped on them."

He stooped, resting one knee against the top step. "There's blood on the porch."

She looked to see what he was talking about. A brown patch marred the surface, then another one and another. "Are you sure it's blood?" she asked.

"Looks like it. Dried blood looks the same in just about every situation. And this one looks to be in the form of a shoe print."

She could think of a number of reasons for the open door and crushed flowers, but the blood worried her. With the way things had been going lately, she decided being on guard now might save them some trouble later.

Brandon must have felt the same. He pulled his weapon. "Stay behind me."

Sonya didn't argue. Brandon used his elbow to nudge the door open farther.

Just as he did, something slammed into it, causing wood fragments to fly everywhere. Brandon cried out and went down. Sonya hit the floor of the porch, terror racing, survival instincts kicking in.

She felt Brandon snag her arm and roll her into the house. He slammed the damaged door behind them and pulled out his phone. He pressed it into her hand. "Call 911."

Blood dripped from his forehead. He had a gash on his cheek. Sonya realized his face had protected hers.

She froze for a split second, then dialed the number.

The operator came on the line. "What's your emergency?"

Sonya sat up. "Someone just shot at us. They're outside in the trees, shooting at the house." She rattled off the address. She turned to find Brandon at the window, pressed to one side, the curtain parted. Her gaze landed on the couch and she bit back a scream. Her muffled whimper caught his attention. She nodded to the couch and he blinked. Into the phone, Sonya said, "There's a woman who needs help. Actually, I think she may be dead."

Brandon left the window and went to the woman, felt for a pulse, looked up and shook his head.

Sonya approached the body and dropped to her knees. She handed Brandon the phone and mimicked his actions in feeling for a pulse even though she knew she wouldn't find one. The blood on the woman's torso said she'd met a violent death. Sonya looked into the open, staring eyes of the victim and felt her throat tighten. "Someone shot her," she whispered.

"And not too long ago," Brandon said. "The blood isn't dry."

Brandon identified himself to the 911 operator and requested the necessary personnel for the crime scene. He handed the phone back to Sonya and let his eyes roam the house. Tension quivered through him and he went back to the window and held his weapon ready.

Sonya shivered and swallowed hard, the hair on her neck spiking. Goose bumps pebbled her skin.

He moved the curtain one more time. "I don't see anyone, but I didn't hear or see a car drive away."

"Whoever shot at us may have just run or had a car parked somewhere else."

"Yes." Brandon stepped toward the kitchen and rounded the corner in a smooth move. Then checked the pantry.

All the while Sonya could see him keeping an eye on her, too. "What is it?" she asked.

"I don't know. We don't dare go out yet, but I don't want any surprises in here, either."

"Surprises?"

"There are two glasses on the counter and a water bottle. The glasses could belong to Ms. Gold and her killer, and she could have poured the water from the bottle. Or the bottle could belong to a third person." He glanced around again. "If the shooter left someone behind…"

"Oh."

Sonya watched as he moved from the kitchen to stand to the side of the entrance to the hallway. She knew if she hadn't been there, he would have probably gone into the back rooms, but because of her presence he was waiting for backup.

That was fine with her. She rose and snagged her purse from where she'd dropped it when they'd tumbled into the house. It took only a moment to locate the small first-aid kit she carried. Packed with only the bare necessities, it still had a good-sized bandage. "Let me stop the bleeding on your head."

He swiped the bottom of his shirt across the wound. "Not yet."

He still wasn't convinced they were the only ones in the house.

She glanced back at the victim and felt sorrow squeeze her heart. Ms. Gold was in her early sixties. A woman who might have held some answers to Sonya's kidnapping. Answers that seemed to be lost forever now. But it wasn't just that. Ms. Gold probably had had quite a few good years left, and someone had stolen those from her. It wasn't fair.

"How long do you think she's been dead?" Brandon asked.

Sonya swallowed hard. "I don't want to touch anything or destroy any evidence, but..." She crouched down beside the dead woman and lifted her arm. It moved easily. "She's not in rigor. I'd say she's just recently been killed." She swallowed. "Like, in the past hour or so."

"Or past ten minutes," he muttered.

"I'm not a medical examiner, so it's just an educated guess, but rigor usually sets in within four hours of death."

"The fact that someone just shot at us tells me that if we'd gotten here a few minutes earlier, we might have interrupted the killer."

"And saved this poor woman's life." Tears squeezed her throat. She blinked and coughed to get rid of the knot. It didn't help much.

"I don't think her killer surprised her," Brandon said. Again, his gaze moved around the room.

Sonya saw what he did. "No sign of a struggle or forced entry."

He shot her a surprised look and she shrugged. She'd picked up a few things by hanging around him.

He nodded. "Exactly. I'm guessing she let the person in and was shot before she could think about what was happening." He aimed his weapon at the hallway. "This place needs to be dusted for prints. My guess is, if Ms. Gold knew the person she opened the door to, the person wasn't necessarily wearing gloves."

"So the killer might have touched something."

"Yes."

A sound from the back made her jump. A muscle in Brandon's jaw spasmed. Never taking his weapon away from the hallway, he pointed to Sonya and motioned her to the kitchen door.

Sonya heard the 911 operator on the phone requesting her attention. She lifted a brow, stood and moved in the direction Brandon indicated. She put the phone to her ear. Brandon backed toward her. Fear swirled in her stomach as she realized he thought someone else was still in the house.

SIXTEEN

Brandon felt exposed. As if he had a big target on his back or his forehead and the killer was laughing at him as he took his time deciding when to pull the trigger. And Sonya…how was he going to keep her safe? He heard her whispering on the phone with the 911 operator.

She backed into the kitchen as a police car pulled up. Brandon kept his weapon trained on the hallway. The back door off the porch was still open. "Stay here." Officers were on the way. They'd have a plan and Brandon needed to be in on it. "Hand me the phone, please."

When she did, he identified himself to the dispatcher and gave his badge number. "I need to know the plan."

"Patching you through to the responding officers."

He heard the click on the line. All the while, he kept his gaze on the hallway entrance. No more noises had come from the back of the house, but that didn't mean he was ready to drop his guard.

A voice came on the line. "Officer Tim Miller."

"Officer Miller, this is Detective Brandon Hayes. Right now, this is your playing field. How do you want to do this?"

"Is the house clear?"

"Just the den and kitchen area. The victim is on the couch in the den."

"So you haven't yet cleared the bedrooms?"

"Right. We're holed up in the kitchen."

"We've got officers approaching now. Others are canvassing the neighborhood."

Brandon's blood hummed.

Ten minutes later, there'd been no more strange sounds and no more flying bullets. Two officers approached the back door, back-to-back and weapons drawn. Three more cruisers had arrived. Brandon opened the door and they entered.

Brandon flashed his badge and focused in on the officer whose name tag read Tim Miller. Miller eyed him. "You're Hayes?"

"I am."

Miller's gaze flicked to Sonya. "Stay with her while we clear the house."

Brandon itched to be a part of it, but he wanted Sonya safe more than he wanted to go looking for anyone who may be hiding. So he stayed and kept his weapon nearby while the officers cautiously headed down the hall.

"Clear!"

"Clear!"

The shouts came from the bedrooms.

Seconds later, Miller came into the room holding a white-and-gray cat. "I think this may have been the noise you heard."

Brandon felt some of the tension leave him.

"Who knew?" Sonya asked.

His gaze snapped to hers. "What?"

"Who knew we were coming here? Ms. Gold is dead because we said something about coming to see her. So who did we tell and who did those people tell?"

Brandon pulled in a deep breath. "I don't know, but we're going to figure it out."

Exhaustion didn't begin to cover how Sonya felt. The shooting and the subsequent questioning by the police had taken their toll. Finding Ms. Gold dead had been a horrifying experience and all she wanted to do was go to bed. But the thought of going home—or even back to Missy's—had terrified her. Then, of course, there was the depressing fact that they no longer had any leads to figure out who'd kidnapped her all those years ago. She tried to push the thoughts aside and focus on her present situation.

Brandon had brought her to his house, planted her on the couch in his den and told her to nap while he fixed dinner. She'd closed her eyes, but knowing he was there—sensing him walk back and forth between the deck, where he grilled, and the kitchen, from where tantalizing smells emanated—stirred her appetite and she couldn't sleep. Instead she'd drifted, enjoying how, despite the danger, being with him made her feel safe.

Safe. She'd almost forgotten what it felt like. The sound of his approaching footsteps lifted her lids. He came out of his kitchen drying his hands on a towel. "Dinner is served."

She rose, walked into the dining area of the kitchen and gaped. Two steaks sat in the middle of the table along with two baked potatoes and a bowl of salad. "How did you do this so quickly?"

He laughed at her expression. "I've been a bachelor a long time. It was either learn to cook or starve."

"I'm deeply impressed."

He flushed. "Don't be. It was really easy."

"Well, thank you. I'm honored you'd cook for me."

He held out a chair and she slid into it. "I heard you order your steak medium well at one of the restaurants we went to, so this one is yours." He stabbed it with a knife and placed it on her plate.

"Perfect," she murmured.

He cleared his throat. "I suppose you want to say a blessing?"

"I'd love to." She bowed her head. "Thank You, Lord, for the food and for continuing to keep us safe. Amen."

"Amen."

She looked up and found his thoughtful gaze on her. "What?"

"Through all of the troubles you've had lately, you haven't lost your faith or blamed God."

She shrugged. "Why would I blame Him? He didn't kidnap me or shoot at me."

"But He could have stopped it."

She sighed. "Of course He could have, but He chose not to. For whatever reason, He's decided to allow this trial in my life at this time, and I'm not going to blame Him for it. I'm just going to ask Him to get me through it. Just because I have some trouble in my life doesn't mean He's not God anymore." She took the bowl of salad and transferred some to her plate, then chose the ranch dressing. As she poured it over her salad, she said, "It doesn't mean I like it, but—" she lifted a shoulder "—it is what it is and I'm going to trust Him to see me through."

"And if you die?"

"Then I die. Again, I don't want to die, but if I do, I pray something good comes from it that turns people to Him."

He frowned. "You're just like them."

"Who?"

"Erica and Max. Jordan and Katie. They all would have the same attitude you have."

She gave a small smile. "It's part of being a believer, a part of who I am."

"Not all believers have that attitude."

"No, I guess they don't. I'm not saying it's easy, but faith is a journey. I think when things are going well, it's easy to have faith. When things are going bad, you have to decide how you're going to react. Are you going to trust God or not?"

"I wish it was that simple for me."

"It's not simple. It's a choice."

"What about how you feel?"

"What do feelings have to do with it? You can't trust your feelings. Feelings can lead you to do or say things you shouldn't. Trust what's true and what's right because whatever is true and right is of God."

He simply stared at her, his mind spinning. "I've never thought of it that way before."

"Maybe you should."

"Maybe I should."

Her smile tipped into a frown and she looked around. "Speaking of Jordan, where is he?"

"Playing watchdog. He knew I was bringing you here, so he's guarding the perimeter."

"Oh, poor thing. It's really hot out there. I hope he's got some shade."

"And a vehicle with good air-conditioning. And you don't have to feel too sorry for him. I made him one of these steaks for later."

She nodded and took a bite. "Delicious."

"Thanks." He looked distracted then blurted, "But don't you *ever* doubt?"

She hesitated and thought about that. Then shook her head. "No, not about who God is or that He's in control."

"Then what?"

"Sometimes I doubt that my faith is strong enough. I get frustrated on occasion and want to whine or throw a temper tantrum and demand my way, but ultimately, it comes down to accepting that this is what it is right now and doing what I can to stay strong in the midst of it."

"Don't you hate the person who's doing this to you?"

"Hate him? No. Want him to stop? Most definitely. And yes, I'm angry and want to see justice done, but I'm not wasting my energy hating someone. What's the point in that?" He stared at her long enough to make her uncomfortable. She wanted to squirm. Instead, she took a few more bites of the steak. "You're a very good cook."

He blinked and looked down at his own plate.

"Oh. Thanks." He lifted his head and caught her gaze once again. "You're amazing."

She flushed. She knew she did because she could feel the heat in her cheeks. How did he do that to her? She never blushed. "Well. Thank you."

"You make me want what you have."

Her heart flipped. "You already believe in God, Brandon."

"I know, but I've been mad at Him for a long time."

"Because of your parents."

"Mostly."

"And the fiancée?"

"Mmm-hmm. Yes." He continued to stare into her eyes.

"What?" she asked.

"I'm thinking that my fiancée leaving me could be the best thing that ever happened to me and I just couldn't see it until now."

Now it was her turn to stare.

He laughed, then shrugged. "I'm learning that there's more to just believing in God. There's the whole faith thing, trusting Him and believing that He has a plan in all of this."

"Exactly. It's not easy, but it's very…freeing, I guess is the word."

"Freeing?"

"Yes. You know. To have an absolute. To believe what God says is true. When you look at life through that filter, it keeps everything in perspective."

For the next few minutes, they ate in silence. Sonya's phone rang and she snagged it from her pocket to see Mrs. Talbot's number on the screen. "Hello?"

"Is this Sonya?"

"Yes, ma'am."

"Well, good. I hope I'm not catching you at a bad time."

"Not at all. What can I do for you?"

"You know when you were here asking all those questions about your mother?"

"Of course."

"I got to thinking about it and seems like I do recall her mentioning something about a phone call she'd gotten not too long before she passed."

Sonya sat up straight. "A phone call. From who?"

"She didn't say, just that she had to make a decision about something and was torn as to what to do. I didn't think much of it. I guess I thought it had to do with planning her funeral. And it may have. But I thought of it and wanted to tell you."

"Thank you so much. I'm glad you did."

"Hope it helps you figure out whatever it is you're figurin'."

"Me, too," Sonya said. "Me, too."

She hung up.

"What was that all about?" Brandon asked.

She told him. "You think it's important?"

"Maybe. Let me think about it."

"I wonder who called her."

He set his fork and knife on the edge of his plate. "Why don't we find out?"

"How?"

"Give me your mother's number and I'll get her phone records. We'll go through the numbers and see who called her the last couple of weeks before she died."

Sonya rattled off the number and he placed a call to whoever it was that could get him the information he needed.

He hung up. "So, let's get you over to Missy's and settled in."

"I think I'll go to Mom's house instead." Sadness gripped her. "One day I suppose I'll have to start calling it my house."

"Do you plan to keep it?"

"I might as well. It's paid for and I have some lovely memories of when I used to visit. We'll see."

"Looks a little small to raise a family there," he said.

She lifted a brow. "Well, since I don't have a family to raise, it's not a problem."

"What about later? Say if you meet someone, get married and start having kids?"

Sonya swallowed. She didn't want to read anything into his words, but she almost couldn't help it. "When—if—I get to that stage, then I suppose my husband and I would have to talk about it and decide what to do."

"So you'd be willing to move?"

She gave him a sad smile. "It's just a house, Brandon."

He stood up and carried his plate to the sink. She looked at her mostly eaten steak and half the baked potato and realized she was full. "I'd be willing to move, yes." Then she frowned. "But I want to be there tonight. I've been thinking that if she left the baby bag in the closet, there may be other things that I've missed."

"But you've cleaned out the house, right?"

"Most of it. But I haven't touched my mother's furniture. You know, her drawers."

"Just the closet?"

"Yes. And not all of that. I stopped when I found the bag."

"What about the attic?"

"No." She grimaced. "I don't like going up there. Anything in the attic wouldn't be worth looking at anyway, I don't think."

"You never know."

"And besides, what would I be looking for? I've

already found the bag, and that was in the bedroom closet."

"So what are you thinking?"

"Whenever Mom got a phone call, she would write down important things on a small tablet she kept in her end-table drawer. I want to see if she wrote anything about that call that seemed to upset her."

"Good thinking. Come on. I'll take you."

"Now?"

"Why not? I want you safe, Sonya, and the only way that's going to happen is if we figure out who wants to hurt you. If you don't want to go to Missy's, then I'm going to make sure you're safe at your mother's."

"Right." She put her plate in the sink. "Don't you want me to help you clean up?"

He laughed. "Naw. That's what my cleaning service is for." He grabbed his keys. "Let's go. I'm impatient to see if we find something." He paused after he opened the door. "Stay here until I check the car out."

"You're going to look for a bomb, aren't you?"

"It only takes one time to make a man a little paranoid."

SEVENTEEN

Brandon pulled into her drive and looked in the rearview mirror. Max had pulled to a stop across the street. He waved and Brandon gave a relieved sigh. Frankie couldn't pull guard duty tonight, so Brandon had had to come up with a plan B. Having contacts and friends that could help out at a moment's notice wasn't something he took for granted, but it was definitely something he appreciated.

His phone rang and he grabbed it while Sonya pulled her things together. It was Holt from the lab. "Hello?"

"Hey there. Somehow I got to be the designated caller."

"About?"

"Ballistics."

"Ah, yes. You want to tell me how, with your love of weapons, you didn't go into that part of forensics?"

"DNA opened up first, but I'm qualified to work

ballistics, too. I just don't advertise it in case they decide they need to do some cutbacks or move people around. I'm happy where I am."

"Right. So what do you have for me?"

Sonya had stilled in the passenger seat and looked at him.

Holt said, "The bullets outside Mr. Bradley's office came from a Savage model 16FCSS Weather Warrior series bolt-action rifle. It's a .308 Winchester caliber twenty-two-inch free-float and button-rifled barrel with—"

"Just the facts," Brandon drawled. "And in English." He knew if he let him, Holt would go on and on about the rifle and never get around to the actual reason he'd called.

Holt quieted then cleared his throat. "Right. The bullets fired at you guys in front of Mr. Bradley's office from the rifle your shooter left behind and the ones fired at the people in the park where Sonya was jogging were a match."

Brandon let out a low whistle. "I was right."

"Yep."

"So why shoot the other women if he was after Sonya?" Brandon mused out loud.

Sonya frowned. Little lines formed above the bridge of her nose and he wanted to reach out and smooth them. Instead, he curled his fingers into a fist and concentrated on Holt's words.

"I wondered that myself. The only thing I could

come up with was that he wanted to cover up the fact he was after Sonya."

"He wanted her to be a third victim in a random shooting," Brandon muttered. "The police would investigate and come up empty on any connection between the three women and chalk it up to a crazy."

"That's my theory."

"It makes sense. Thanks, Holt."

Brandon hung up and interpreted the rest of the conversation for Sonya, but it looked as though she'd gotten the gist of it. Her face paled and she swallowed hard. "Those women in the park were shot because he was after me," she whispered. "And one died because—" She pressed her fingers to her lips and a tear slipped down her cheek.

"It's only a theory, Sonya. We don't have any proof."

"But it makes sense," she said. "I didn't have any connection to either of those women. None." She sniffed and swiped at her eyes.

He was almost ready to take her in his arms when she slammed a fist against the dash. "I still don't hate whoever is doing this," she said, "but I sure do want to see him in jail, where he belongs."

"Let's go inside." He climbed from the car and saw Max watching them with a look of concern. Brandon waved that all was fine and followed Sonya to the front door.

She paused, key in the lock. "I still haven't picked up my car from the hospital."

Brandon reached around her and unlocked the door. He knew he was big enough to block any bullets headed her way, but he wasn't in the mood to get shot again. He ushered her inside and shut the door behind them.

Sonya dropped her purse on the foyer floor on her way into the den. She paced from the mantel to the sofa and back. "I want this over with. I want my life back."

"I know. And we're making progress. It's just going to take time."

She touched the wound on her throat and then her fingers slid over the butterfly bandage on his cheek where the flying wood from the door had gashed him. "I'm tired of us getting hurt, tired of being afraid you—or someone else that I care about—is going to get killed because of me."

Brandon's fingers gripped hers. "I'm glad you care about me." Heat suffused her cheeks, but she refused to look away. She did care about him and wanted him to know it. "But," he said, "this situation isn't your fault. You're not responsible for the actions of whoever is doing this."

She sighed. "I know it's not my fault in that I'm not the one going around hurting people, but if I hadn't started looking for Heather Bradley, none of this would be happening and Ms. Gold would probably still be alive."

He grimaced. "Maybe she would. But if I understand things correctly, her death didn't take God by surprise."

Sonya stilled. "No. That's true. It didn't. None of this has taken Him by surprise."

"So let's focus on what we need to do to end it."

Sonya took a deep breath and nodded. "Okay."

"Now, where's your mother's room?"

"This way."

Sonya opened the door to her mother's bedroom. She'd saved this area for last, knowing it would take all of her strength to get through the memories, to wade through the grief and accept that her mother was gone from this side of heaven. The only thing that made the grief easier to bear was the fact that she would be reunited with the woman she loved one day for all eternity.

Hopefully, later rather than sooner as the person trying to kill her seemed to be determined to make happen.

She went to the end table and pulled out the drawer. Papers, pens, hair ties, face cream, a fingernail file.

Her notepad.

Sonya pulled it from the drawer and sat in the chair at the vanity table next to the door. She flipped through the yellow legal pad. Notes about doctors' appointments, things her mother had wanted to tell Sonya.

Tears welled at the sight of the handwriting. Brandon's hand settled on her shoulder and she sniffed. "Sorry."

"It's okay."

She nodded and flipped through the pages. "I don't see anything," she whispered. "This was a dumb idea."

"It was a great idea," he countered. "It's never—" His phone rang and he pulled it from his pocket. Sonya started over at the beginning of the notepad, hoping she'd missed something. And she did. Two pages stuck together. With a gentle tug, she separated them and stared.

"'Blackmail,'" she read aloud. "'Sonya.'" Just the two words written one on top of the other.

"Stay put, Spike. I'll be right there." Brandon hung up. "What did you say?"

"The word *blackmail* and my name underneath. Look." She turned the notepad so he could see it.

"Why would your mother write that on her notepad?"

"I have no idea."

"You think her agitation could have been because someone was blackmailing her?"

The thought sent knives of pain through her heart. "There was nothing to blackmail her about."

"How much money did she leave you?"

Sonya shrugged. "About a hundred thousand in savings bonds. And the house is paid off."

"So not an exorbitant amount, but enough that could be attractive to someone who didn't make but twenty or thirty thousand a year."

"I guess." Sonya swiped a stray tear and saw the frown between his eyes. "What's wrong?"

"Spike's been arrested."

"For what?" she gasped.

"Trespassing and resisting arrest are the charges. Apparently Spike was snooping around your house, looking in windows and such. A neighbor called it in. An officer drove by and saw him, tried to ask him what he was doing, and Spike panicked and ran. The officer chased him, caught him and took him downtown."

"When did all that happen?"

"Right before we got here." He held his phone up. "Spike just got his phone call."

"Then go. You need to help him. I'll just stay here and see if I can find anything else." She sighed. "I need to go through her stuff anyway."

"Are you able to do it?"

"I'm able." She gave a small smile. "The memories are good. I just miss her."

He pulled her into a hug and squeezed. "You're going to be all right, Sonya."

She leaned back and looked up at him, ignoring the pull on the stitches. "When you say it like that, I believe it."

"Good." He placed a light kiss on her lips, a quick touch that offered comfort and expressed his concern for her. She also sensed a passion carefully held in check. She shivered and relished the moment.

When he pulled back, she asked, "That was lovely, but what about the no-kissing thing?"

He stopped and frowned. "Oh. Right. I must have been out of my mind." He ran his thumbs over her cheeks and gave her one last hug. "We need to talk, but it'll have to wait. I'll be back as soon as I take care of Spike. Max is right outside."

"All right. Thanks."

Brandon left and she locked the door behind him. They needed to talk? About? The kissing thing, probably. She went back to her mother's room and looked around. She sighed and went to the dresser. She opened it at the same time that her cell phone rang.

She snagged the device from her pocket and recognized the Bradleys' number. "Hello?"

"Am I speaking with Sonya?"

The female voice took her aback. "Yes, this is she."

"This is Ann Bradley."

For a moment, Sonya couldn't get her throat to work. Finally, she said, "Hello, Mrs. Bradley."

"I overheard Don talking to someone on the phone. He said that you're definitely Heather."

"Yes, ma'am. That's what they said."

"Well, I…I've been doing some thinking. Even a little praying."

"I see. About?"

"You, of course."

"Oh."

"And I've decided that I want to welcome you into the family. That is…if you're even interested in being a part of our family."

Sonya swallowed hard. "I want to know you. I do. But I really want to know why I was kidnapped and who would do such a horrible thing."

"Do you think you can get past that? What if you never find out?"

Sonya thought about that for a minute. "Then I suppose I'll have to accept it and move on."

"Do you think you can do that?"

"I don't know. I suppose I would always wonder."

"Would you come to my house so we could talk?"

Sonya considered it, then thought about Max outside. "I really shouldn't leave. Someone still wants me dead."

"I could send a car for you."

"No, but…"

"But what?"

"I would tell you that you could come over here, but being around me can be dangerous. I have someone watching the house, but it's still not safe. I think we'll just have to wait until this is all over."

"I'll take my chances. Will you let your guard know I'm coming?" Sonya paused, undecided. A sigh filtered through the line. "Please, Sonya, I need to talk to you."

"All right, I'll let Max know. He'll probably ask for some identification."

"I'll have some."

"See you soon." Sonya hung up and felt her stomach swirl with a mixture of anticipation and dread. Inviting her birth mother into the house of the woman who'd loved and raised her for almost thirty years seemed almost wrong. But Sonya had been stolen from Ann Bradley and that wasn't her fault. She missed her mother, she always would, but that didn't mean she couldn't get to know the woman who'd given birth to her.

She called Max and told him the plans.

Brandon found Spike in the holding cell. He'd have to stay there until he could have someone bring the money for bond. Brandon wanted to know more before he decided to pay it himself. He didn't think Spike would be able to afford it and he knew his mother couldn't. He looked the teen in the eye. "What were you doing at Sonya's house?"

Red crept into the boy's cheeks and he shrugged.

Brandon sighed. "Come on, man. Talk to me."

"I wasn't going to break in and I wasn't going to hurt her if she was there."

"Okay, I believe you."

Spike's head snapped up. "You do?"

"Yes." Brandon did. Mostly. But he kept that niggling of doubt to himself and refused to let it show on his face.

Spike's shoulders slumped. "If I tell you, you will laugh your head off."

"Laugh?"

Spike nodded.

"Try me." Brandon couldn't imagine what was going through his young friend's mind.

"I was…" He mumbled the last part of the sentence.

"Say it again. Clear so I can understand you."

Spike lifted his head and his dark eyes bored into Brandon's. "I was trying to be like you. I was doing what a detective does. You know, check things out, seeing if your lady was all right. Keeping an eye on the place. Only someone saw me and called the cops."

Brandon pinched the bridge of his nose. All the time and effort he'd put into helping Spike had paid off. And Spike had just laid the biggest compliment ever on him. Brandon blew out a breath. "Well, dude, I'm not going to laugh."

"You're not?" Skepticism showed.

"Nope. But I am going to get you out of here."

"How?"

"I'm going to pay your bail. How else?"

For the first time since Brandon had met Spike, he thought he saw a sheen of tears appear. Spike blinked and looked away. "Aw, man, you don't have to do that. I deserve to be here."

"For what?"

"For being so stupid."

"You weren't being stupid. You were being a kid." Probably for the first time in his short life. "All right. Hang tight. I'll be back."

"Yo, Hayes, you got a minute?"

Brandon turned to find Hector waving at him. "Yeah. Coming."

"I'll be at my desk."

To Spike, Brandon said, "I mean it. I'll be back."

Spike nodded and leaned his head back against the cell's wall. Thankfully, he didn't have any cell mates, and Brandon would see to it that he didn't.

Brandon hurried to find Hector. He found his partner and seated himself across from him even as he pulled out his phone and shot a text to Max. How is she?

Just fine. Quiet. Mrs. Bradley's coming for a visit.

Now, that was interesting. He looked at Hector. "Hang on a sec while I finish this text to Max."

"Sure." Hector went back to his computer.

Brandon sent a reply. Did she say why?

No, just that Mrs. B. wanted to see her. To talk. OK. Keep me updated. Hope to be back soon.

10-4.

Brandon set his phone on the desk in front of him. "Okay, I'm finished for now. What's up?"

"I've found out something rather interesting."

"What's that?"

"You know how you were all skeptical about the death of Mrs. Bradley's sister?"

"Yes."

"I decided to dig into her death a little further. The M.E. did rule her tumble down the stairs an accident, but there was one little detail that you don't know."

"What?"

"She'd just had a baby not too long before her death."

Brandon froze as his mind clicked through this new information. "When was the baby born?"

"I don't have an exact date, but the M.E. noted in the chart, 'a recent birth, probably within the last couple of months.'"

"But no one's said anything about her having a baby. Where's the child?"

"She gave it up for adoption."

Brandon lifted his eyes to lock on Hector's. "Are you thinking what I'm thinking?"

"I'm thinking there's a lot more to this story than we know."

Brandon nodded. "What if Heather Bradley— Sonya—is really Ann and Don's niece?"

"Why keep that a secret?"

"Why don't we ask him? You got his number handy? I've got it on my phone somewhere…." He started scrolling through the list.

Hector pushed the file over to him and Brandon flipped through it until he came to the personal-information section, where he found Don Bradley's number.

The man didn't answer. Brandon left him a message asking him to call him back.

He looked at Hector. "Okay, so Sonya said her mother got a phone call she was concerned about. Said it agitated her. We requested her phone records with Sonya's consent. Where are they?" He asked the question almost absently as he moved files and papers to see if they'd been buried.

Hector reached into the bin on the corner of his desk and handed them to him.

"Thanks." Brandon started going through the list of numbers, looking for anything that might pop out at him. Fortunately, the list was short and he had a good idea of the time frame he needed to look at. He started at two weeks before Mrs. Daniels's death.

He pulled his keyboard toward him and opened the software that would allow him to input a phone number and trace it back to the owner.

Ten minutes later, he stopped and stared. Hector looked up. "What is it?"

"Why would someone from the Bradley household be calling Sonya's mother before Sonya even knew anything about the diaper bag and birth certificate?"

EIGHTEEN

Sonya opened the door to Mrs. Bradley and waved at Max, who gave her a two-fingered salute. "Come in."

Mrs. Bradley followed her into the den. "Would you like anything to drink?"

"No. Thank you." Mrs. Bradley twisted her hands together in a nervous gesture and took a seat on the couch under the window.

"What made you decide to call me?" Sonya asked.

Mrs. Bradley sighed. "A lot of different things. The main one being that if you're really Heather, then I can't ignore that."

"The DNA test was very conclusive."

"Yes, I know."

"Is that why you're here?"

"I came to find out what you want."

Sonya bit her lip. Then sighed. "I really don't want anything. At least not from you. All I wanted was to find out who Heather Bradley was. I wanted to find out why my mother would have her birth certificate and baby bag in her closet. So I hired someone to find out." She stood and paced to the mantel, then back. "Then someone tried to kill me." She held her hands up, beseeching. "Now I'd like to find out who wants me dead. Is that too much to ask?"

"But who?" Mrs. Bradley leaned forward and some of her resistance seemed to fade.

Sonya eyed the woman who was her mother. "You tell me. It's only when we started poking into your family that the assaults started."

Mrs. Bradley pursed her lips. "I can't think of a soul who would do such a thing."

Silence dropped around them like a scratchy blanket. Sonya shifted. "Look, if this is making you uncomfortable, we don't have to do this. I know you don't want to believe I'm your daughter and that's okay."

"You're not my daughter."

"Even though the DNA test proves I'm Heather?"

"Yes, even though."

"I'm confused. If I'm not your daughter, then why does the DNA prove I'm Heather?"

Mrs. Bradley hesitated then rubbed a hand across her eyes. "Sonya, I believe you're Heather. And you were supposed to grow up as Heather Bradley, but I didn't…give birth to you. We adopted you."

Sonya froze and let that statement sink in. "Okay." She shook her head. "Can you please explain?"

Mrs. Bradley nodded. "It's a rather long and crazy story, but you're actually my niece. We adopted you from my sister."

"The one who died?" Strangely, Sonya felt nothing. No shock, no sorrow, nothing. She wondered if she had maxed out on emotional overload.

"Yes."

Sonya swallowed hard. "Did she really fall down the stairs?"

Mrs. Bradley teared up. "Yes, I think she really did. The carpet was messed up at the top and she was always warning me or guests to be careful." She gave a sad shrug. "I'd been by to see her that morning and she was fine physically. Emotionally was another story. Anyway, later that afternoon she was dead."

"So she was my birth mother," Sonya whispered.

"Yes."

"Who's my birth father?"

The woman shrugged. "I don't know. She never told me. All she said about him was that he was married and they weren't going to see each other anymore. And he didn't want the baby."

"So you adopted Heather. Me."

"Yes."

Sonya's head started to throb.

* * *

Brandon's phone rang. "Hello?"

"This is Don Bradley. You called?" The short clipped words took Brandon by surprise.

"I did. You sound busy. Is this a bad time?" Brandon tried to be gracious even though the man had called him.

"No." Don cleared his throat. "No. Sorry. I just had a rough meeting. What can I do for you?"

"We've come across some more information and need your input."

"What is it?"

"I'm just going to come right out and ask. Was Heather your niece and not your daughter?"

Silence rippled across the phone line, and Brandon almost wished he'd gone to see the man in person. Then a heavy sigh filled his ear. "Why do you ask?"

Brandon told him what Hector had discovered. More silence. "I see."

"What do you see?"

"Sometimes when you keep a secret for so long, you start to believe the lies you told."

"What lies, sir?"

"I'm just not sure I see the point in—"

"A simple DNA test comparing Sonya's to your wife's sister's will be all it takes to find out. We're also going to want a DNA test to compare yours and your wife's to Sonya's."

"Why would you need ours?" The man's wariness came through loud and clear.

Brandon was bluffing. He had no grounds to stand on to ask for a DNA sample, but if he had the DNA from all parties involved, maybe he could get some answers for Sonya. "To find out who she's related to without question. Would you be willing to come in and offer a sample?"

Another heavy sigh. "I don't need to offer a sample. I guess the truth always finds a way to surface, doesn't it?" He paused. Brandon wondered if he was going to speak again. Finally, the man said, "Yes, she's my daughter." He hesitated again. Again, Brandon waited him out. "But," Don finally said, "she's not my wife's."

Brandon got it. "You had an affair with your sister-in-law."

"I did."

"I see."

The man sighed. "It wasn't an ongoing thing. It was actually a one-time thing. Ann was at the gym like always. Miriam stopped by and we talked, had a few drinks. She started crying about being lonely—" The pause drew out and Brandon could almost picture the man gathering his thoughts.

"And?"

"I went to comfort her and she kissed me."

"And you didn't push her away."

"No," he said flatly. "I didn't push her away."

"So when she came and told you that she was pregnant with Heather?"

"I freaked out. But," he sighed, "Ann and I had been trying to have a baby forever. Once I calmed down and thought about it, I realized this might be our chance." Another pause as though he was searching for the words. "Each month that went by without a positive pregnancy test sent Ann deeper and deeper into a depression. She dealt with it by spending more and more time at the gym, working out, getting fit, eating healthy. She thought if she kept her body in perfect shape, then it would happen. She'd get pregnant."

"But she didn't."

"No. And now I had a baby on the way with her sister."

"What did she say when you told her?"

"We didn't tell her. Miriam went to Ann and told her she was pregnant, but refused to tell her who the father was, just saying he was married, but wasn't in the picture anymore. She said that she couldn't raise the child by herself and would Ann and I be willing to take the baby."

"And Ann said yes."

"Not at first. She was afraid Miriam would change her mind, but Miriam didn't want the baby. She made that clear. She said she was too young to be a mother and if Ann wouldn't take it, she was going to see an adoption agency. I pressured Ann that we should do this and Ann finally agreed."

"Did Mrs. Bradley ever find out that the baby was yours?"

"No. Miriam would never say anything. She knew Ann wouldn't forgive her for that. Ever. And Miriam needed Ann." He snorted. "Or at least the money Ann poured into her."

"You resented the money she gave her sister?"

"Well, her father had cut her off for a reason. She'd made some pretty bad choices. Her parents had had enough of it and refused to give her any money."

"But Ann did."

"Yes."

Interesting. Brandon asked, "So she gave you the baby."

"She did. She had a home birth and a midwife. She just handed Heather to Ann when it was over. My lawyer took care of everything else. It was a private adoption with very little paperwork. But everything was straight up and legal."

"Who did she name as the father? The father would have had to agree to the adoption."

"Not if you claim you don't know who the father is."

Everything sounded as if it had been done legally, just as he'd said.

"So who would benefit from having Sonya out of the picture?"

"Now, that I don't know." He cleared his throat. "And I would very much appreciate it if you would keep all of this confidential. I don't want Ann to find out. Ever. It would devastate her." Another slight pause. "And our marriage. My life would be over. Do you understand what I'm saying?"

"Unfortunately, I do understand, but I honestly can't make any promises. But I won't mention it unless I have to."

The man's silence conveyed his unhappiness with Brandon's answer, but Brandon wasn't going to make promises he might not be able to keep.

Brandon hung up with Mr. Bradley and flipped back to the front of the file. They'd put every scrap of information about the case into one place. He turned over page after page after page. And stopped when he came to the pictures of the car with the rifle. The one the shooter had used in the parking garage. The forensics team had gone through the vehicle with a fine-tooth comb and had photographed everything.

One picture stopped him.

"Hey, Hector."

"Yeah?"

"This guy worked at Gold Star Gym, right?"

Hector looked over his shoulder. "Yes. So?"

"So I've seen this emblem before." He pointed to the gold star on the man's identification badge.

"Where?"

"On Mrs. Bradley's gym bag."

"Oh, boy."

Brandon had another thought. "Check and see if Mrs. Bradley showed up for her appointment with her trainer at the gym the day Ms. Gold, the nanny, was killed. I'm calling Max and telling him to get inside with Sonya."

Hector got on his phone while Brandon called Max. When Max got on the line, Brandon said, "I don't have time for details. Just get inside with Sonya. Mrs. Bradley looks good for the one who's been trying to kill her. Be careful. Hector and I are on the way."

He stood as Hector hung up the phone. The grim look in his eyes didn't bode well. "What is it?"

"She never showed up. In fact, she hasn't been to the gym for the past two days. And guess who her trainer was?"

"Our shooter?"

"The one and only."

Sonya's phone rang and she flinched. "Excuse me a moment, please."

"Of course," Mrs. Bradley said.

She grabbed the device. "Hello?"

"Sonya, this is Brandon. Are you all right?"

Her heart thudded at his voice and his face came immediately to mind. "Yes, I'm fine."

"Max texted me that Mrs. Bradley was coming by. Is she there yet?"

Sonya glanced at her visitor. "Yes, we were just talking. I've learned some pretty interesting things."

"Okay, don't react to what I'm going to tell you, all right?"

Sonya swallowed, but hoped she kept her face expressionless. "Okay."

"I've asked Max to come inside with you. It looks like Mrs. Bradley is the one who hired someone to kill you."

Sonya couldn't help the small gasp that slipped out. She glanced at the woman who was watching her, head tilted, eyes narrowed. She quickly turned away. "Okay. Why do you think that?"

"The shooter was her trainer at the gym. He had a bit of a shady past and we think she hired him to kill you. And, Sonya—"

"Yes?"

"Don Bradley just told me that he and Ann adopted you from Ann's sister."

"I know," she whispered. "Right before your call, Ann revealed I was Miriam's daughter. But she never learned who my father was."

"Sonya..." Brandon hesitated. "Don Bradley *is*

your biological father. He had an affair with Ann's sister." Sonya gasped. Her knees weakened.

"I know it's a shock," Brandon said, his compassion ringing through the line. "I'm heading that way now."

Sonya felt a small kernel of fear start to replace her shock. "That's fine."

There was a knock on the door. Sonya crossed the room and glanced out the window. "Max is at the door."

"Let him in," Brandon said. "I'm already in the car. I'll be there in less than ten minutes. I've also got backup on the way."

Sonya reached for the lock and wondered if Mrs. Bradley would try to stop her. She unlocked the door and twisted the knob. Mrs. Bradley didn't move.

Max stepped in and shut the door behind him.

Now the woman stood. "What's going on?"

Max eyed her. "That's what we want to know. Why are you trying to kill Sonya?"

Mrs. Bradley gaped. "What? Try to kill her? Are you out of your mind?"

The door burst in. Max started to turn and a gunshot rent the air. Max went down. Sonya screamed.

NINETEEN

Sonya dropped to her knees beside Max, who lay facedown. He groaned and tried to roll, then dropped back to the floor. "Max!"

A hard grip on her upper arm yanked her to her feet. The gun in her face sent terror racing through her. She lifted her eyes to the man behind the weapon and gasped.

Don Bradley.

"What are you doing?" Sonya cried.

"Taking care of things." He turned to his wife.

The woman stood pale and shaking, her brown eyes wide, blank.

Shock.

"Get in the car." Don shoved her toward the door and Sonya almost tripped over Max.

"What about Max?"

Another hard shove in the small of her back sent her stumbling toward the door. "Hopefully, he'll die where he is." He aimed the weapon at Max. "Another bullet ought to take care of that."

Sonya whirled and hurled herself at him. "No!" She slammed into the arm that held the gun and Don went to his knees as he lost his grip. The weapon skittered across the hardwood floor and hit the edge of the brick fireplace.

Sonya dived for the gun. "Ann, run!"

A hard grip wrapped around her ankle and yanked. She lost her balance and rolled. Don regained his footing, grabbed the gun, aimed it at her and pulled the trigger.

The loud crack echoed. Sonya felt the bullet whiz past her face and froze. Don approached and shoved her up against the wall, fingers wrapped around her throat. "Get. In. The. Car."

Stars whirled in front of her eyes and darkness flirted at the edges of her mind.

Then she was free and gasping in air. Her already bruised throat throbbed in time to her heartbeat. His fingers tangled themselves in her hair as he dragged her to the door.

Ann still stood staring, eyes wide and blank.

Don shoved with the gun. "Get in the car, Ann. The backseat. I'm going to take care of this."

Ann walked out the door.

Pain ratcheted through her head, her throat, her neck. Everywhere. He pulled and she had no choice but to follow. Within seconds, Ann slipped into the backseat and Don opened the driver's door. "Crawl over."

The black BMW was large and roomy, and Sonya had no trouble slipping into the front passenger seat. All the while aware of the gun pointed at her. She glanced in the rearview mirror, the side mirror. Where was Brandon?

She looked at the clock. The entire incident in her house had taken less than five minutes.

Don held the gun in his left hand while he started the car with his right. "Just had to butt in," he muttered. "You just couldn't leave the past in the past, could you?"

She stared at him. "All I wanted to do was find Heather Bradley."

"And all I wanted was for her to stay gone."

Brandon pulled to the curb behind Max's car. Sonya's scream and subsequent click of the phone disconnecting had sent terror shooting through him.

Blue lights at the end of the street flashed the impending arrival of other officers. Brandon reported in his position, knowing the dispatcher would inform the other officers nearby.

Ann Bradley's vehicle was parked in Sonya's driveway. Max's car still sat at the curb. "Why isn't Max answering his phone?" Hector muttered.

Worry beat at Brandon. He wondered the same thing. Max hadn't answered his phone for the past seven minutes.

Jordan's brand-new SUV pulled up the rear.

Brandon climbed from his car and heard Hector's door slam. He pulled his weapon and held it close as he approached the front door. He rapped his knuckles on the wood.

No answer. "Sonya?"

Jordan motioned he would check the garage.

Hector stayed close. "You think she's in trouble?"

"She screamed. Then the phone cut off."

"Could have been a mouse."

"That would be good news."

"Yeah, I don't think so, either."

Jordan returned. "Garage has a vehicle in it." Brandon rapped on the door again, then twisted the knob.

Unlocked.

He stepped inside. "Max!" He strode to his friend, the bloodstain on his back sending another bolt of fear through him. "Call for an ambulance."

Jordan was already on the phone by the time Brandon dropped to his knees to feel for a pulse. Faint, but steady. Relief made him shudder.

Then he spotted a cell phone wedged under the side of Max's abdomen. He pulled it out and held it up. "It's Sonya's," he told Jordan.

"That's not good."

Hector and two uniformed officers returned to the den. "All clear," Hector said. "How's he doing?"

"He needs a hospital," Brandon said.

An officer waved at Brandon. "We just got a 911 call from a neighbor on this street. A Mr. Tobias. Shots heard."

"Did he see anything?"

"No, said he was in the back of the house and thought it might have been a car backfiring, but then he decided to check it out. By the time he got to the window, he saw a car at the end of the street, but couldn't make it out."

Brandon ran a hand through his hair. "How am I supposed to find her?" He paced, thinking.

"Officer? Hey, let me through!"

Brandon turned. "Who are you? Do you know something about what happened?"

"I'm Sonya's neighbor across the street. Paul Lehman. There was a guy who took Sonya and another woman. He had a gun."

"You saw him?"

"Yeah. He shoved them in a big black BMW and took off. Sonya was one of those women, but I didn't recognize the other one."

That stopped him. "A man?"

"And two women."

"Sonya dropped her phone, so that's not going to help us. And you say he had a gun?"

"Yes, but he was trying to hide it. By the time I went to get my own weapon, he was gone."

"Do you have a weapon on you now?"

"No, I'm not stupid. Once I saw they were gone, I locked it back up."

Brandon thought of Max. "Whoever he is, he's definitely not afraid to shoot someone."

An ambulance screeched to a halt and two paramedics headed for the house, directed by one of the uniformed officers.

"I don't suppose you got a plate?"

Mr. Lehman grimaced and shook his head "No, sorry. Not all of it, anyway. I think the first letter was an *H*. I couldn't get close enough to see it by the time he was pulling away."

Brandon squeezed the man's shoulder even as his anxiety skyrocketed. "I want to know who was here."

"We'll start questioning the other neighbors," Hector said. "And I've already put a BOLO out on a black Beemer."

"Can we get the helicopter?" Jordan asked.

Brandon pulled his phone out and called Christine, his sergeant. In terse, precise sentences, he filled her in on the situation. "I'm running out of time. He's got her and another woman, presumed to be Mrs. Bradley, in his car. I don't have a clue who he is or where he'd take them."

With only a slight pause, she approved the helicopter request.

All they needed now was to find the black BMW with three people. He started praying.

* * *

Sonya gripped the door handle as Don sped down the highway. In the rearview mirror, Sonya could see Mrs. Bradley slumped in the backseat.

"Why are you doing this?" Sonya whispered.

"I spun some pretty good half-truths and lies to your boyfriend, but it's only a matter of time before they figure everything out."

"Figure everything out? What do you mean?" His knuckles whitened on the steering wheel and Sonya moved her fingers to the door lock. "You said you wanted me to stay gone. Do you know who kidnapped me when I was a baby?"

"Yes."

"Because you set it up?" She took a shot in the dark even as she noticed they were on I-85 and going north.

He flinched and Mrs. Bradley gasped. Sonya took another look in the mirror and noticed the woman sitting upright and paying attention. Some of the shock had worn off and her eyes appeared clear. And narrowed. Sonya didn't think Don had noticed. He moved into the left lane to pass a slower vehicle. The needle on the speedometer inched up. Suddenly, things started clicking for Sonya as her mind put a few more pieces together. "You killed Ms. Gold, didn't you?"

"You were going to talk to her."

"And she's the only other person who knew the truth."

"Yes," he said.

"She took me, didn't she?"

"I paid her to walk into the nursery and walk out with you. That's the one thing she managed to do right in this whole thing."

"Were you blackmailing my mother?"

He snorted. "No. Rebecca was. She'd broken into the lawyer's office and gotten your mother's name as the adoptive parents. She figured out that you didn't know you were adopted and threatened to tell you. From what little I gathered, your mother didn't want you to know."

Sonya closed her eyes. Her mother wouldn't succumb to blackmail. She'd been going to tell her. Sonya now knew exactly why her mother had been so agitated before she'd died.

"What did Ms. Gold hope to get by blackmailing my mother?"

"Money, of course."

"Why after all this time?"

"I have no idea. I should have killed her long before I did."

His cold-blooded statement sent chills racing up her back. "I'm still not clear on why you didn't want me. You adopted me from your sister-in-law. Why would you do that if you only wanted me to disappear?"

"Because my wife insisted. And I had to do whatever it took to keep Ann happy." He glanced in the rearview mirror. "Right, Ann? Had to keep you happy." His lip curled, and the disgust Sonya saw on his face made her swallow. "When I paid Rebecca to take you from the nursery, I told her I didn't care what she did with you, just to get rid of you."

Sonya flinched. "So she put me up for adoption."

"No, she sold you to some lawyer who found two people desperate enough for a baby to part with their life savings."

"My parents," she whispered.

"Yes."

Sonya knew why he was being so forthcoming. He wasn't planning to let her ever repeat this crazy story. Her mind frantically worked, trying to figure out the best way to deal with him while looking for a way to escape.

Keep him talking. Keep him talking. "Who was the man who tried to kill us? You hired him, right?"

"He was Ann's personal trainer. He was always looking for a way to make some quick and easy cash."

Sonya clenched her fingers into fists. "Where are you taking us?"

"I haven't figured that out yet. Now be quiet and let me think."

She ignored his order for quiet. "How did you know to come to my house?"

"Ann said she was going to go see you. I followed her. After the phone call with your boyfriend earlier, I could see he was putting it all together. Hopefully, I've fed him enough lies that he'll be confused for a little while. Long enough for me to put a plan together, anyway."

"You're going to kill us," she whispered. "You're going to kill your wife?"

A strangled sound came from the backseat.

Don shot her a fierce look. "I'm not going to kill my wife." He glanced in the rearview mirror. "We're going to take an overseas trip. Finally find a little place in the Caribbean and have a nice quiet life. Doesn't that sound good, Ann?"

"Yes, dear." Her monotone voice worried Sonya, but Don didn't seem to notice. He gave a small satisfied smile.

"But you're going to kill me," Sonya stated.

The smile slipped from his face. "Your presence could ruin everything. You simply know too much. Especially now."

The man wasn't thinking straight. "I got a phone call before you got there. Brandon told me they suspect that Mrs. Bradley is the one who wants me dead. You don't think they won't be looking to talk to her, do you?"

He stilled, a muscle jumping along his jawline. "What makes them think she had anything to do with it?"

"You just told me that the man you hired was her trainer. It didn't take them long to connect the two."

"So they figured that out, did they?" he murmured. "That idiot. I told him how to cover his tracks and he ignored me. Just goes to show you that in order to get something done right, you usually have to do it yourself." He pulled into the back of his office building. "Get out my door. There's no one down here this time of day. We're going to use the service elevator and go up to my office."

Sonya frantically searched for an escape route, a weapon she could use on the way in, anything. The gun pressing into her lower back discouraged her from trying anything immediately. "I can't believe my own father would do this to me. I'm your blood child. What threat am I to you?"

"Shut up." He pressed her toward the entrance. Ann hadn't moved from the backseat. He looked at his wife. "Come on, Ann. I need you to come with me. This will all be over soon enough."

Without hesitation, Ann climbed from the vehicle and followed them into the building. Confusion swept over Sonya. Why would he bring her here? It seemed like the most obvious place for Brandon to look for her.

Then again, he didn't yet realize that Don was the one behind everything. "Does your wife know you had an affair with her sister?"

The gun whipped around and caught her on the side of her head. "I said shut up!"

Pain ricocheted through her. A scream escaped and darkness threatened. She fought it off even as her knees buckled and she went to the ground.

When her vision steadied, she saw Ann staring at her husband, her face devoid of color. Don had his attention on her. "It's not true, Ann. She's lying. She'll say anything right now."

Sonya lurched to her feet and turned to run while he had his eyes and his weapon turned away from her.

She took two steps before a hard hand twisted in the back of her shirt and jerked her to a halt. She barely kept her feet when he yanked her around and shoved her toward the door. She slammed into it and leaned against it, praying she wouldn't pass out.

She noticed the security camera in the corner of the building and looked straight at it. Don gave a low laugh. "I've already thought of that camera, Sonya. It's no problem to erase the video. Now go."

TWENTY

Hector's phone rang and Brandon shot him a look. His partner answered and listened while Brandon tapped the dashboard, impatience eating through him.

As soon as Hector hung up, Brandon pounced. "What?"

"The chopper spotted a black BMW entering the parking garage where Don Bradley works."

Brandon blinked. "Don Bradley? What does he have to do with this?"

"Maybe he's the one who took them?"

"But why?"

"Who knows? Maybe he's got his own reasons."

"But would he dare take them to his office? It's too simple, isn't it?"

"I'd say we're going to have to check it out."

"What if it's a decoy?" He paused then checked his weapon. "Call for backup to head that way. I have a very bad feeling about this."

"His business is textiles, right?"

"Yes."

"If you wanted to get rid of someone without a trace and you owned a textile business, how would you do it?"

Brandon shuddered and a wave of nausea swept over him as he thought. "Textile companies use acid for various things. I'd say there's probably enough in the building to hide a murder."

Hector flinched and stepped on the gas. Brandon prayed even as he got on the phone and formulated a plan. He filled his boss in. "I need help here, Christine. I need blueprints of the building. I need a way to clear the building without letting Don know we're onto him. I need a SWAT team and a hostage negotiator. Send them all and send them fast."

"They're on the way."

"And I am, too."

Ignoring the intense throbbing at the base of her skull, Sonya pressed her palm hard against the door. If he was going to kill her, someone was going to find out she'd been here and she was going to leave evidence behind.

Her throat ached at the thought of dying and never knowing if she and Brandon could have had something wonderful. She hated the pain her death would cause him.

But maybe he'd figure it out soon.

She prayed for Max. She prayed for them all.

She'd seen Mr. Lehman looking out his front window. He'd seen her get into the black BMW, and she knew once Max was found, a full-on investigation would kick into play.

Once inside the building, Don directed her down a long hall past several other doors. They turned, right, then left, and by the time he finally stopped and let go of her hair, she knew she'd have a hard time finding her way back should she manage to get away from him. He gave her another hard shove toward a door marked with a hazardous symbol. "Step to the side."

"What are you doing, Don?" Mrs. Bradley finally spoke, coming out of her shocked stupor.

Don jumped and stared at her as though he'd forgotten all about her. Sonya's nerves twitched and she shifted. The weapon swung back to her even as he addressed his wife. "I have to take care of things." He handed her his keys. "I want you to go up to my office and wait for me."

She ignored the keys. "Take care of what? What about Sonya? Why does she think you're going to kill her?"

"I'm not going to kill her," he soothed her. "Sonya and I have business to take care of. Then we'll join you."

"What kind of business? Why do you have a gun? You shot that man at Sonya's house. Why?"

"Will you stop asking questions and do what I asked you to do?" His shout echoed through the area. His wife flinched and narrowed her eyes.

Then her shoulders slumped and she turned without another word.

"No, wait!" Sonya cried. "You can't do this!"

Ann paused, but didn't turn.

Don ignored her and simply reached over to punch in the code to the room. The door opened.

He shoved the gun into her rib and moved her inside.

Sonya frantically scrambled for an escape plan. Ann followed her inside.

"What are you doing? I told you to go upstairs." Ann stared at him. Don shook his head. "Fine. Fine. I'll just have to deal with you, too."

She didn't offer a response, but didn't leave, either.

Don moved behind his desk and picked up a key. "Now, it's time to end this once and for all."

"What are you going to do? If you're going to shoot me, shoot me!" Sonya knew at such close range, her chances of ducking were slim, but if he started shooting, maybe the noise would bring someone running.

"Shoot you? Of course not."

She stared at the gun and wondered if he'd lost his mind. "Then what?" she whispered. Why had he brought her here if he didn't plan to kill her? Confusion swept through her.

"You'll see. And I promise, it's relatively painless."

Brandon and Hector arrived at the parking garage only seconds ahead of the other officers. "There's the black BMW."

"You think it's his?"

"No idea." Brandon walked over to the vehicle and placed a palm on the hood. "It's hot. Hasn't been here long."

"First letter on the license plate is an *H*. Let's get a search going. We'll have to lock down the building. No one in or out."

Brandon nodded, his brain spinning, fear for Sonya wanting to short-circuit his thoughts. When Hector finished giving orders and putting the plan into motion, Brandon eyed the door with the combination code. "He wouldn't take them through the building, where anyone would see them."

"The basement?"

"Where does that door go?"

Hector tapped a few keys on his phone. "I had the blueprints emailed to me." More tapping. "Looks like it does go into an area that's sealed off. A hazardous area."

"That's where we need to go. I need the code.

Who would have it?" he muttered. Then looked up. "The security officer. Where is he?"

Within seconds, they had the man at the door, punching in the code.

Sonya kept her fear under control. Barely. Mrs. Bradley had once again lapsed into a catatonic state. She'd backed up to the wall and slid down to sit on the floor. Now she stared, a blank, empty stare that said she'd suffered too much and had mentally checked out.

Sonya felt horrible at having exposed Don's affair with his sister-in-law in such a blunt way, but she'd been desperate and hoped the knowledge would spur the woman into helping her.

Instead it had sent her into a place in her mind that Sonya wasn't sure she'd ever come back from.

Don kept the weapon on her. The room they'd entered had a sign on the door that read Authorized Personnel Only. He shoved her toward one of the two matching steel chairs. "Sit down." She sat. With the gun still trained on her, he glanced into the other room toward his wife. "Ann!" The woman didn't move. Didn't blink. With a curse, he shook his head. "She's always been weak. Weak but loaded."

"So you married her for her money?"

"Of course not. I loved Ann. I would have done

anything for her. But when she couldn't have children, she changed."

"So why not just leave her? Why kidnap the only child she'd ever have and send her deeper into depression?"

"Because the child was mine. And her sister's. And if her sister ever said a word, I was done." His steady hand never wavered and the gun never moved from her as he backed toward a file cabinet and opened the second drawer with his free hand. "You see, I signed a prenup. If Ann ever decided to divorce me, I would get nothing."

"And if Miriam ever said anything, Ann would divorce you without hesitation," she whispered. He blinked but didn't answer. He didn't have to. "You killed Miriam, didn't you?"

Don pulled a large hunting knife from his desk drawer.

Fear crawled through her. "What are you going to do with me?" Relatively painless or not, she wanted to know.

He set the knife on his desk and pulled out a roll of duct tape. Sonya knew he'd just confirmed what she'd known all along. He might not plan to shoot her, but he did plan to get rid of her.

"You don't have to kill me." She felt the quiver in her voice, but was glad it didn't come out in her words. She wanted to be strong. To believe help would come.

But help might be a long way off. She was going to have to rescue herself. *Lord, I need You to help me stay calm and think clearly. But I wouldn't mind some help if You could please send Brandon. Let him figure out where we are.*

"Yes. Yes, I do." He approached, duct tape in one hand, weapon in the other.

The coldness in his eyes made her shudder. "What does it matter now?" she cried. "You didn't want Ann finding out that you had the affair with her sister. Well, now she knows. What else is there that you don't want anyone to find out? What threat am I to you? Let me go and we'll forget this ever happened." She cast a glance at the still-open door. Don was either too preoccupied or too cocky to bother with shutting it. Ann hadn't moved. If she could make it to the outer door, she had a chance.

"Don't even think about it. I can't let you go. He'll find out and I'll be on the streets." She almost didn't catch the low muttered words.

"Who'll find out?"

"It doesn't matter now."

"Who?" she pressed.

"My father-in-law," he shouted. "The dictator." He moved toward her with the tape. Sonya stood and whirled to stand behind the chair.

Don stopped and blinked as if he couldn't believe she'd actually just defied him. The gun lifted. "I was trying to do this the nonmessy way, but—"

Sonya gripped the edges of the chair and in one smooth seamless move lifted it and crashed it into his outstretched arm.

Don screamed and the weapon clattered to the floor.

Sonya bolted through the open door.

His curses behind her filled the air as she ran, not knowing where she was going, but praying it was toward safety.

"Did you hear that?" Brandon lifted a hand.

"It was faint, but it sounded like someone yelling," Hector said.

"This way." Brandon moved down the hall, made a turn and came face-to-face with another hallway that branched off into two directions. He stopped. "Which way? It's a maze down here."

Hector glanced at his phone. "The blueprints aren't much help. Unless we know exactly where they are, I don't know which direction to take." He lifted his head. "You hear anything else?"

"No." Brandon listened. "Wait. Footsteps?"

"Maybe, but from where?"

Brandon shook his head. "I can't tell." Frustration filled him. Which way? "We can't just stand here." The officers shifted behind him. He turned. "Fan out. Split up. Check every room, every closet.

I think we have the element of surprise, so be quiet and be careful. He's armed. Go." They went, their footsteps making little sound on the hall tiles. He looked at Hector. "Let me see those blueprints again, will you?"

Hector handed him the phone. Brandon moved his finger across the screen then zoomed in on the area where they now stood. "Okay, there's a large area. Looks like a warehouse type space. Over here are offices—"

Officers headed back their way, guns held, faces grim. "All clear back this way."

Brandon handed the phone back to Hector and motioned toward the next hall. "Then we go this way."

"Stop!"

Brandon froze. "You hear that?"

"Yeah. That way."

"I said stop!"

Sonya heard his furious shout as she raced down the hallway, her tennis shoes slapping against the tiles. A glance over her right shoulder sent terror shooting through her. Don followed right behind her, eyes full of fury, burning holes into her back while his right hand gripped the hunting knife. Fear spurred her faster.

She turned a corner, then another. She had no idea where she was. A large door at the end of the hallway beckoned. With an extra burst of speed, she reached it and yanked on the handle.

Locked.

And then he had her.

He wrapped his fingers around her upper arm and glared down at her. "You have to know the code," he snarled.

Sonya kicked out and caught him in the knee as she spun from his grip. With a howl of pain, he struck out and landed a hard fist against her cheek.

Pain blinded her for a brief moment. Long enough for him to punch in the code and shove her through the door.

She stumbled and fell to the floor. "Leave me alone!" Scents assaulted her. The smell of vinegar nearly overpowered her. Her gaze darted even as her brain processed the new environment. A large open area with a high steel ceiling. Blue barrels filled with whatever chemicals were used in the textile industry.

And no other exit that she could see.

Don yanked her to her feet and pushed her toward a set of steel steps that led to a second floor. A matching steel balcony ran the length of the fifty-yard wall.

He had no weapon but the knife, she realized. He hadn't taken the time to grab his gun before coming after her. But he was strong. Much stronger than she. And the knife was wicked-looking and sharp.

Her face throbbed. Her head ached and nausea churned in her belly. "Why are you doing this? They'll find you and figure it out and you'll go to jail for murder. Stop now and you won't spend the rest of your life in prison!"

"Shut up!" He gave her another shove. She fell against the step. Pain shot up her shin. He grasped her hair once again and twisted. She cried out and her vision dimmed.

"Move!" She winced at his shout. Dizziness hit her and she fought it off.

Sonya regained her footing and took the stairs slowly, her brain spinning, her body aching. Barrels of acid below, the unknown above. At the top of the stairs, with his hand still gripping her hair, he paused as though to get his bearings. She realized he was undecided about what to do.

The acidic vinegar smell nauseated her, and her head pounded, begging for relief. Tears leaked from her eyes and prayers slipped from her lips.

A sound from below pulled her captor to a halt. "Sonya!"

Brandon's frantic cry had never sounded so sweet.

TWENTY-ONE

Brandon stared up at Sonya, trapped by Don Bradley, who shielded himself with her body, a knife at her throat. Her throat that had just begun to heal from the last time she'd been held in a similar position. "Don't come any closer. Get out! Get out!"

Hector moved behind him to his left, and other law-enforcement personnel swarmed behind him.

Brandon stepped forward, his eyes locked on the man and not the woman he realized he'd give his life for. "Let her go, Don."

"Not a chance. I'm not going to prison, so just back off and let me get out of here."

"Where do you think you can go that you won't be found?"

"I have money. I have resources. I'll manage or die trying. Now move! Get them out!"

Brandon saw movement behind Don. Someone had found another way in. He frowned. He didn't remember another entrance or exit on the blueprints.

But there was an elevator that came from up above. Officers must have utilized it.

But shooting Don in the back risked the bullet passing through and hitting Sonya. He had to talk this man down.

Sonya's terrified eyes followed him as he took another step toward the duo. "What are you going to do, Don?"

"I don't know! I have to think. How did you find me? How did you know I'd come here?"

Brandon ignored his questions. "You didn't plan this, did you? You're going by the seat of your pants." He took another step. And another.

"Stop! I'll kill her." He pressed the blade tighter, and Sonya's eyes widened as she went up on her tiptoes. "See that acid down there? I don't even have to cut her. I'll just throw her in it. Now back off!"

Brandon froze as he saw exactly what the man was talking about. Three barrels of acid, lids removed, were directly under the steps where Don had Sonya. All he had to do was give her a shove and she'd land in one of them. He shuddered. "Please, Don. Think of your wife. Ann's been through so much."

"Ann," he spat. Then his anger faded and sadness etched itself in the grooves of his face. "I used to love her, you know. But then she changed, became so sad. And I couldn't do anything to make it better."

"That must have been terrible." Brandon interjected as much sympathy as he could muster. He just needed to distract the man long enough to get Sonya away from him.

"So awful he turned to my sister and had a child with her." Ann's quiet voice came from behind Don.

He spun, the knife dropping slightly as he pulled Sonya around with him.

A shot rang out and Don's right shoulder took the bullet.

Sonya screamed as the knife scraped across her already wounded throat. Don flung her against the rail and she went to her knees. He fell beside her, his eyes bright with pain. His hand reached for her and she rolled.

Over the edge.

For one weightless moment she hung suspended. A scream welled and terror filled her. Her fingers grasped, scrambling for a hold.

"Sonya!"

Brandon's cry echoed as she gripped the edge of the steel landing. Her feet dangled over the barrel of acid.

Behind Don, who lay bleeding and writhing against the pain, she saw Ann on the ground, hands cuffed. Brandon's wide eyes appeared above

Sonya's and his fingers locked around her wrist. Don gave a roar as he surged up and brought the knife around, aiming it at Brandon.

"Watch out!"

Another shot rang out and Don dropped. Officers raced to him, kicking the knife away and cuffing him.

Brandon gave a grunt and pulled on her wrist. She swung a leg over the landing and rolled into his arms. Sonya held on while tremors racked her.

"It's okay. You're all right. I've got you," he whispered.

Chaos reigned around them while he held her. After a moment, she gained a semblance of control. "Is he dead?"

She didn't recognize her weak, shaky voice. But she wanted to know the answer. Pulling away, she looked around his shoulder and saw Don staring at her. Two officers stood over him, weapons drawn and pointed at his head. He blinked. "You didn't have to do this," she whispered.

"I didn't know what else to do," he rasped. "Ann would have divorced me. I thought getting rid of you would shut down the questions." He swallowed. "I couldn't lose it all."

"And yet, that's exactly what you've done."

He closed his eyes and fought for his next breath.

She saw Ann being led away by two officers.

Paramedics entered and headed for Don. Brandon pulled her to her feet. Her knees wobbled and she leaned on him, grateful for his support, his nearness.

"Come on." He placed a kiss on her forehead and tightened his arm around her shoulders. "Let's get out of here. We can do our statements soon enough."

Sonya followed him, her mind in turmoil. "I want to see Ann."

"She's been arrested for shooting her husband."

"He was going to kill me. She should get a medal."

"She's lucky she wasn't shot, too. I wonder how she got the gun."

"It was Don's," Sonya said. "I managed to knock it out of his hand when I ran."

"But he still had the knife."

"Yes."

"I guess she knew a shortcut to where he was holding you. I don't remember seeing it on the blueprints."

"It doesn't matter now."

Once outside, the police let them through. A paramedic raced up and Brandon let her go long enough to get her throat looked at and rebandaged. The paramedic ushered her into the back of the ambulance. Sonya explained the original injury and the woman shook her head. "You've had a rough time of it, no doubt. The good news is, no stitches required for this new injury. Looks like the knife hardly touched you."

Sonya nodded her thanks. "It's really only a graze. It stung, but didn't really cut me." *Thank You, Lord.*

She looked for Brandon and found him a few feet from the ambulance. "What about the other bumps and bruises? You should go to the hospital and get checked out."

"No. I'll pass. I have enough medical knowledge to know Don didn't do any lasting damage."

"Thank God for that." He helped her down and led her over to his car, where Peter and Jordan stood. Peter grabbed his brother in a bear hug. "Are you all right?"

"Yeah, I'm fine. Or I was until you hugged me and set off the throbbing in my shoulder again."

Peter grimaced and stepped back. "Sorry."

"I'll live."

Jordan hugged Sonya. "Glad you're all right."

"Me, too. Thanks." Sonya shuddered and Brandon squeezed her fingers. "How's Max?" The man had never been far from her mind or her prayers.

"He's going to be fine," Jordan said. "The surgery to remove the bullet went well and he's already fussing about being stuck in the hospital. Erica's practically sitting on him to keep him from checking himself out."

Sonya breathed a sigh of relief. "Good. I'm so glad this is all over. Mostly at least."

"What do you mean?" Brandon asked.

"I still have some questions." She gave a light shrug, then winced at the movement. "I don't suppose they matter, but I would love to know why all this happened now. Why would Rebecca Gold wait so long?"

"She might not have been able to find you," Brandon said. "Didn't you move quite a bit?"

"Yes. A lot."

"So maybe once she got up the nerve to try to do the blackmail scheme, she couldn't find you until recently."

"Maybe."

"So Ms. Gold tracked down Sonya's mother and gave her the bag and birth certificate as proof she knew they had adopted Sonya," Peter said.

"That's why Mom was so agitated at the end," Sonya whispered. "She wanted to tell me, but couldn't find the courage to do so."

"And then we mention tracking down the nanny in front of Don Bradley and he has no choice but to find her first and kill her."

Sonya shuddered. "It's all so needless."

Commotion behind her caused them to turn. Paramedics wheeled Don Bradley from the building. He had an oxygen mask on his face, an IV in his arm and leg irons clamped around his ankles. Straps held his arms to the gurney.

Sonya blinked and tried to register the fact that the man whose blood she carried had wanted her dead. Had, in fact, killed others to keep his secrets. He'd had no desire to reunite with the child he'd given up so many years ago. It hurt, but Sonya realized she was much better off. Her parents had been wonderful and raised her to be strong in the Lord.

If she'd grown up as Heather Bradley, she'd be an entirely different person. "Thank You, God," she whispered.

Peter clapped his brother on his shoulder. "See you Sunday at Mom and Dad's?"

Brandon seemed to waver, and then his face hardened. "No, not yet."

Peter sighed and without another word turned on his heel and headed for his car.

Brandon pulled her aside, leaving the others talking and speculating about the day's events. "It's over."

She nodded. "I know."

He leaned over and kissed her. "I want a chance with you, Sonya."

"And I want one with you, Brandon. With all my heart that's what I want."

He pulled back and looked at her, wariness in his eyes. "I hear a 'but' at the end of that sentence."

She bit her lip and fought the tears that wanted to fall. "Tell me how I can help you get past the bitterness you feel toward your parents." She stroked his cheek. "Tell me how to help you."

"Why is this so important to you?" A muscle ticked in his jaw.

"Because I'm not perfect," she said.

He blinked. "I know that. I'm not, either."

"But you expect your parents to be. Will you expect me to be, too?"

He frowned. "What are you talking about?"

"Your parents made mistakes. Bad mistakes. Mistakes that haunt you today, but they've asked for forgiveness. They've asked for a second chance. What about when I mess up and make a mistake? One that makes you angry or hurts your feelings? Are you going to hold a grudge and refuse to forgive me?"

"Sonya, of course not."

"Then let it go, Brandon. Because until you do, I can't be with you."

Brandon stared as the woman he thought he might very well love walked away from him. But her words still rang like gongs in his ears.

Two days later, Brandon sat at his desk at Finding the Lost, staring out the window, contemplating the last words Sonya had spoken to him.

Was she right? Of course she was.

"You going to let her go?"

Brandon jerked and spun his chair to find Jordan in the doorway. Jordan's mild words sliced across his heart.

"No. No, I'm not."

"So what are you going to do?"

"I'm going to talk to Peter and see if he'll help me with my rehab."

At Jordan's raised brow, Brandon gave a sad chuckle. "I'll explain later. Right now, I have to find my brother."

He left Jordan smiling after him as he grabbed his keys and raced from the building.

Twenty minutes later, he knocked on Peter's door.

When Peter opened it to find Brandon on his doorstep, he raised a brow. "What are you doing here?"

"Looking for you."

"I'm not hard to find. Come on in."

Peter grabbed a bag of chips from the coffee table and held them out to Brandon. "Lunch?"

Brandon grimaced. "How did you do it?"

Peter didn't have to ask. He set the bag of chips aside and sank onto the sofa. "It wasn't easy, but I have a mentor. Someone who prays for and with me."

Brandon dropped into the recliner and noticed it

was new. "That's enough to keep you away from the drugs?"

"Yes. It doesn't matter what time it is, day or night, if I call, he answers."

"And does what?"

Peter gave a self-deprecating smile. "Talks me off the ledge. Makes me laugh. Meets me for coffee. Whatever it takes to help me walk away from the temptation."

Brandon swallowed hard. "I'm sorry."

Peter frowned. "For what?"

"I'm sorry it wasn't me. I should have been there for you like that and I wasn't."

Peter shrugged. "No. It was better to have a stranger do it. If you had been the one telling me some of the stuff Nick has, I would have hated you, turned my back and never talked to you again."

"Oh." Brandon thought about that. "Then I'm glad it wasn't me."

Peter gave a short laugh. "No, we're better off just being brothers and friends."

Brandon sucked in a deep breath. "Well, as my brother and friend, would you help me understand how you forgave them?"

Peter sighed. "Get comfortable. This is going to take a while."

Brandon lifted the footrest and crossed his arms. "Where do I start?"

"With a 'want to' attitude."

Brandon thought about that. "Okay. I want to. I really, really want to." And he found he did. Not just because of Sonya, but for himself. He was tired of the anger and the bitterness. He wanted a life of hope and forgiveness. He wanted the life God had planned for him right from the start. A life that included Sonya. His throat tight with emotion, he nodded. "Yeah. I'm ready."

Two months later

Brandon sucked in a fortifying breath and knocked on his parents' door. Eating crow wasn't on his list of favorite foods, but he knew he was doing the right thing. That made it a bit tastier. He smiled as he thought about his brother. Peter had taken joy in encouraging him and praying with him. And surprisingly Brandon had, too. And now it was time to talk to his parents.

The door opened and his mother stood before him, her mouth formed in a perfect O.

"Hi, Mom."

The surprise didn't leave her expression, but at least she was able to find her voice. "Brandon." She stepped back. "Will you come in?"

He hated the hesitation in her voice. "Thanks." He stepped inside and looked around. It wasn't the home of his childhood, but one he'd been to occasionally over the past ten years they'd lived in it. "Is Dad here?" He'd thought he would be, but sometimes his father took an extra shift at the garage.

"Yes. He's in the den watching television."

"Do you mind if I talk to you two?"

Curiosity, wariness and hope all flickered in her eyes. "Of course you can."

He followed her into the den. His father, who hadn't even turned fifty yet and still had a head full of dark hair, sat in his recliner. He looked up when Brandon entered. Shock made him blanch. "What are you doing here?" He glanced at his wife, then back to Brandon. "If you're here to cause us more pain, just get out."

Brandon winced. "I'm not, I promise."

His father picked up the remote and clicked the television off. He frowned. "Then what?"

"I came to say I'm sorry—and to ask you to forgive my stubbornness, my hardheaded selfishness." His pulse pounded. Had he waited too long? Was it too late?

His mother gasped and walked around him to sink onto the couch. "Don't play with us, Brandon. My heart can't take it."

Brandon sighed and his heart tightened as he realized how terribly he'd hurt these two people. Yes, they'd hurt him, but they were actively working on becoming better people. They were trying to atone for their past mistakes. "I'm not playing.

I've been talking to Peter over the past two months and listening to him. Actually listening. He's filled me in on all the changes you guys have made and the fact that you're sincere about wanting to put this family back together."

His mother slipped her hand into his and looked into his eyes. "We're serious, Brandon. We know we were wrong in the past and there's nothing we can do to change that. But we're still young." She gave a sad smile. "Younger than we should be to have a kid your age, but we want to be a part of your life if you'll let us. Please don't let it be too late."

For the first time in years, Brandon hugged his mother. She clutched his shoulders and began to sob. Brandon felt his own tears start to flow and realized Sonya was right. He'd needed to do this as much for himself as he did for his parents.

Another arm slipped across his shoulders. He lifted his head and found himself staring into his father's tearful, red-rimmed, joy-filled eyes. "Thank you, son."

Brandon nodded. "So we're going to start over? No hard feelings, no bringing up the past. Just a fresh start."

"A fresh start." His dad smiled. "A family reunion."

"Of the best kind." Brandon cleared his throat.

"I want to spend time with you guys, but there's a woman I need to go see."

"Sonya," his mother whispered.

"Sonya," Brandon agreed.

"Tell her she's welcome to join in the family reunion, too," his dad said with a watery grin. "On a permanent basis."

Brandon laughed, feeling as if he'd just shed a hundred-pound weight from his shoulders. From his soul. He headed for the door. "I may just do that."

TWENTY-TWO

Two months. Sonya crossed the day off on her calendar. She hadn't heard from Brandon in two months. The longest months of her life.

She'd awakened early for a Saturday morning and now sat at her table sipping her first cup of coffee for the day. She'd worked six days straight this past week and had the next three days off. She actually dreaded them.

She didn't normally work so much, but with Brandon's sudden absence in her life, she needed the work to take her mind off the fact that she missed him terribly.

Lord, I lift him up to You again. I don't understand how my heart could be so entangled in another's this fast, but please continue to show him how much he needs to forgive and how much You love him. And as impossible as it seems, how much I love him.

She'd known him all of a month the day Don Bradley had kidnapped her from her home, but what a month that had been. She'd fought for her life and lost her heart to love in the process.

Her doorbell rang and she debated whether she felt like answering it or not. When it rang a second time, she set her cup on the table and rose.

At the door, she peeked out.

And gasped.

Brandon stood on her front porch.

When he rang the bell for the third time, she swung the door open. "What are you doing here?"

He stepped inside and kissed her. Hard. Then sweet and gentle. Sonya kissed him back, the past two months of loneliness and missing him expressed in her heartfelt response.

When he lifted his head, she saw a sheen of tears glistening in his gaze. "I've missed you."

"Well, that was some kind of hello." She grinned. "I've missed you, too."

He tapped her nose with his index finger. "I'm glad. Do you mind if I come in?"

"Please do." She stepped back and he shut the door behind him. "Come on into the kitchen. I've got coffee."

He followed her and seated himself at the table. "You were right."

She blinked at him. "About?"

"Forgiveness."

"With your parents."

"Yes, and Krystal, my ex-fiancée."

"You've been hurt, Brandon. It's only natural you'd build up some walls and reservations."

"But I don't want them anymore. They're not worth holding on to. Those walls were hurting every relationship I have. Thanks to you, I finally realized what I was doing. Thanks to Peter, I think I've managed to get rid of those walls."

Joy swept over her. He looked lighter. Happier. And at peace. "You've forgiven your parents, haven't you?"

He nodded. "They're good people. They were just too young to have so much responsibility. And they didn't have a lot of help. On my mother's side, my grandparents disapproved and refused to help and my father's parents had already passed." He shrugged. "My mom and dad did the best they could. They're actually pretty amazing if you stop and look at how far they've come and everything they've *overcome*. They beat the odds and are still together. Once I stopped judging, I was able to start seeing things from another perspective. One of compassion and understanding."

Tears filled Sonya's eyes. "I'm so glad."

"We're human. We're not perfect. I'm definitely not, but I believe you're just right for me." He swallowed hard. "I don't know where we're headed, but I want to find out. I know I don't want to spend another day without you in my life."

Sonya flung herself into his arms. "I'm so glad for you. For me. For *us*." She laughed.

He laughed with her. "I've got to be honest with you, Sonya. I want to see you in a white dress, surrounded by flowers and friends, walking toward the front of the church. If you get what I mean." He flushed and shuffled his feet. "If that's not what you want, or not what you want with me, please tell me now."

"I want it, Brandon. I want it more than anything. With you. Only you. These last two months have been horribly lonely without you."

He hugged her tight again. She pressed her nose into the warm skin of his neck and inhaled. His musky scent filled her senses and she felt at peace. She was home. He was the reason God had led her to Finding the Lost. "I love you, Brandon. I know it's fast, but I do. I really do."

"Since when does love have a time limit?"

She giggled. "I like your reasoning."

"So do you think we can do the dating thing for a little while?"

"Absolutely. At least for a week or so."

He threw his head back and laughed, then wrapped his arms around her to pull her close. He placed his lips on hers and Sonya couldn't wait to see what the future held. She thought of how pleased her mother would be that she'd met such a wonderful man. Her father would give his stamp of approval, for sure.

And for Sonya, that was enough.

Enough to make her smile.

EPILOGUE

Thanksgiving
Eighteen months later

Brandon lifted his head after saying the blessing and looked around the Thanksgiving table. A wave of emotion flowed over him and he knew he had a lot to be thankful for. His bride of one year glowed as she passed the mashed potatoes to Max.

Brandon sent a prayer of gratefulness heavenward as he did every time he looked at her. He still had a hard time believing she wore his ring on her finger, but she did. The gold band on his left ring finger fit snugly. He'd already gotten used to wearing it. Took pride in wearing it.

Erica held her newborn son while Max began to heap his plate with food. "Are you hungry, dear?" Erica asked, a hint of teasing sarcasm in her tone.

Max flushed. "Not any hungrier than your dad over there." He transferred the spoonful of dressing to his daughter Molly's plate, then lifted a brow as though asking if he had her approval now. Erica laughed.

Brandon's father had helped himself to a large chunk of turkey. "I'm not shy. I'm starving. I skipped breakfast so I could fill up here."

Brandon grinned and Sonya winked at him. He could see the joy in her gaze along with something else. Curious, he looked closer but couldn't put his finger on it.

Peter looked healthy and happy and joked with Spike. The two had hit it off from the moment they'd met. "So, bro, have you managed to beat Spike yet?" Brandon asked, coating his question in teasing innocence.

Peter's smile slipped into a scowl. "Let's not go there. He only wins because he cheats."

"I do not," Spike protested. The grin on his face said he wasn't too upset about the accusation. They both knew the truth. Brandon had hopes Spike would get a basketball scholarship to college. Spike's mother looked on with an indulgent smile.

Ann Bradley sat quietly on the other side of Sonya. She hadn't said much since the day she'd shot her husband. When he'd been killed in a prison-yard fight, she'd withdrawn even more into her protective shell. But she loved Sonya and seemed happiest when they were together.

Sonya passed him the bread without taking any. He looked at her and his heart skipped a beat. She looked pale. Her lip curled and she slapped a hand over her mouth. She exchanged a look with Erica. "Excuse me," she mumbled. She jumped up and raced from the suddenly quiet dining room.

"Sonya!" He bolted after her, but thought he could hear Erica laughing. Why would his sister laugh at Sonya's obvious distress?

He reached the hall bath and knocked on the locked door. "Hey, are you okay?" The sound of her being sick made him wince. "Oh, baby, do you think you picked up a virus?"

The door swung open. She turned back to the sink to rinse her mouth. Tears leaked down her cheeks. She grabbed a toothbrush and toothpaste. "No, it's not a virus." She gave a hiccuping laugh and brushed her teeth.

He waited for her to finish. "It's not? Then something you ate?"

She turned and patted his cheek. "I haven't eaten yet."

"You've been working hard all morning getting everything ready. Your blood sugar is probably low." He gripped her fingers and pulled her into the hall, ready to lead her back into the kitchen. "That's probably the problem."

"Actually, this problem is going to take about seven more months to solve."

"Seven—" Confusion, then realization, flashed in his eyes. He gave a whoop, then pulled her into a crushing hug. When he released her, she saw the tears in his eyes. "I'm going to be a dad?"

"Yes."

"And you're going to be a mom?"

"That's generally the way it works." She grinned.

He laughed and hugged her again. "Sonya, how long have you known?"

"Just for a little while. I'm about eight weeks along, I think. I have a doctor's appointment on Monday."

"A doctor's appointment? You *are* a doctor." She'd finished up her last semester just after their wedding.

She laughed. "I'm not that kind of doctor."

"Well, I'm going with you."

"Of course you are. That's why I scheduled it on your day off."

He grinned and his eyes danced. The last time she'd seen him so giddy had been on their wedding day. "God is good."

"He sure is," she whispered. "Even in the bad times."

He pushed a lock of hair back behind her ear. "It took some bad times to bring us together."

"Exactly."

His finger reached out to trace her lips. "I remember the first time I saw you, I wanted to see you smile."

"It was hard to find a smile during those days." Her lips curved up. "It's easier now."

"I love you, Sonya."

She wrapped her arms around his waist. "And I love you. We're going to have a great life together. You, me and the baby."

"Babies," he said.

She giggled. "Let's get through this one first."

"Absolutely. But know this. No matter what the future holds, as long as we're together, we'll be fine."

"Hey, are you guys all right?" Erica asked. She'd come into the hallway without either of them noticing.

Max and Molly appeared behind her, then Peter. Then Ann and Brandon's mother and father.

Ann Bradley. Her aunt. She'd pleaded self-defense to shooting her husband and had won. Frankly, Sonya didn't think the prosecution had tried very hard to build a case against her. And now she was a part of the family.

Their growing, rapidly expanding family.

Brandon grinned at his sister. "How would you like to be an aunt?"

Erica blinked, then grinned. "I'd love it!"

"I'm going to be a grandma again?" Brandon's mother pushed her way through the growing crowd to hug Sonya. His father did the same. "Oh, my goodness. This is wonderful."

Sonya looked into her husband's moist eyes. "It's the best thing ever." She clapped her hands. "Now, let's eat. I'm starving!"

Laughter filtered back to her as everyone headed back to the kitchen. Sonya couldn't help the tears that dripped from her cheeks. Sheer happiness filled her, and she offered a prayer of thanksgiving to the One who'd made it all possible.

And she smiled.

* * * * *

Dear Reader,

Thank you so much for joining me on Sonya and Brandon's journey to solve an old crime and find love at the same time. I had a great time plotting their story and putting them in crazy, dangerous situations.

I seem to find myself writing a lot about forgiveness and finding joy in Jesus. I think that's because, as Sonya pointed out, we're not perfect, we make mistakes and we all need forgiveness—and second—and third—and fourth chances.

This is the last book in the Family Reunions series. I hope if you haven't read the first two, you'll find them online or at your local Christian bookstore. Or Walmart. If you'd like to email me, my email address is lynetteeason@gmail.com. You can also find me online at www.lynetteeason.com and on Facebook at www.facebook.com/lynette.eason. I would love for you to sign up for my newsletter if you're interested in keeping up with me and future releases. You can find the sign-up box on my website.

God bless you and may the peace of Christ be with you.

Until next time,

Lynette Eason

Questions for Discussion

1. Brandon's parents' actions caused him to grow up with a lot of emotional scars. What do you think about him still holding on to his anger even when his parents have apologized and reached out to him?

2. Sonya came home to take care of her mother and in the process put her own dreams on hold, including becoming a doctor. What do you think this says about Sonya?

3. Describe Sonya's personality and how you pictured her as you got to know her throughout the story.

4. Do the same for Brandon's.

5. Sonya found out she'd been adopted and then found out she'd actually been kidnapped as an infant. She's determined to find out the truth and who wants her dead. What would you have done in Sonya's shoes?

6. Brandon and Sonya are falling for each other even as they're working together, but Brandon doesn't date clients. At least that's what he keeps telling himself and Sonya. But Sonya

makes it hard for him to stick to his policy of no client dating. What did you think about his policy? Did you agree with it?

7. Brandon is determined to keep Sonya safe. Little by little, they figured out the story behind Sonya's birth and subsequent kidnapping. Who did you think the villain was? Were you surprised by who the villain was?

8. Who was your favorite character and why? What was it about that character that drew you to him/her? His/her faith? The struggles that he/she overcame?

9. In regards to your favorite character: Was there something in that particular character's life that you found you could relate to? What was it and how does it pertain to your life?

10. Did you have a favorite scene in the book? What was it? Do you find you enjoy the suspense scenes or the slower-paced romantic ones more?

11. What did you think about Brandon's relationship with Spike? Do you know anyone who works with at-risk youth and who's made a difference in their lives?

12. What did you think about Brandon's work with at-risk youth?

13. Brandon learned things about himself and his relationship with God. How do you think this will affect him from now on?

14. Why do you think it was so hard for Brandon to forgive his parents and yet he was able to offer forgiveness and second chances to others in his life?

15. Do you think Sonya was right to tell Brandon they couldn't be together until he found a way to forgive his parents? Why or why not?

16. What do you imagine the future will hold for Brandon and Sonya?

LARGER-PRINT BOOKS!

GET 2 FREE
LARGER-PRINT NOVELS
PLUS 2 FREE
MYSTERY GIFTS

Love Inspired®

Larger-print novels are now available...

YES! Please send me 2 FREE LARGER-PRINT Love Inspired® novels and my 2 FREE mystery gifts (gifts are worth about $10). After receiving them, if I don't wish to receive any more books, I can return the shipping statement marked "cancel." If I don't cancel, I will receive 6 brand-new novels every month and be billed just $5.24 per book in the U.S. or $5.74 per book in Canada. That's a savings of at least 23% off the cover price. It's quite a bargain! Shipping and handling is just 50¢ per book in the U.S. and 75¢ per book in Canada.* I understand that accepting the 2 free books and gifts places me under no obligation to buy anything. I can always return a shipment and cancel at any time. Even if I never buy another book, the two free books and gifts are mine to keep forever.

122/322 IDN F49Y

Name	(PLEASE PRINT)	
Address		Apt. #
City	State/Prov.	Zip/Postal Code

Signature (if under 18, a parent or guardian must sign)

Mail to the Harlequin® Reader Service:
IN U.S.A.: P.O. Box 1867, Buffalo, NY 14240-1867
IN CANADA: P.O. Box 609, Fort Erie, Ontario L2A 5X3

**Are you a current subscriber to Love Inspired books
and want to receive the larger-print edition?
Call 1-800-873-8635 or visit www.ReaderService.com.**

* Terms and prices subject to change without notice. Prices do not include applicable taxes. Sales tax applicable in N.Y. Canadian residents will be charged applicable taxes. Offer not valid in Quebec. This offer is limited to one order per household. Not valid for current subscribers to Love Inspired Larger-Print books. All orders subject to credit approval. Credit or debit balances in a customer's account(s) may be offset by any other outstanding balance owed by or to the customer. Please allow 4 to 6 weeks for delivery. Offer available while quantities last.

Your Privacy—The Harlequin® Reader Service is committed to protecting your privacy. Our Privacy Policy is available online at www.ReaderService.com or upon request from the Harlequin Reader Service.

We make a portion of our mailing list available to reputable third parties that offer products we believe may interest you. If you prefer that we not exchange your name with third parties, or if you wish to clarify or modify your communication preferences, please visit us at www.ReaderService.com/consumerchoice or write to us at Harlequin Reader Service Preference Service, P.O. Box 9062, Buffalo, NY 14269. Include your complete name and address.

ReaderService.com

Manage your account online!
- Review your order history
- Manage your payments
- Update your address

*We've designed
the Harlequin® Reader Service
website just for you.*

Enjoy all the features!
- Reader excerpts from any series
- Respond to mailings and special monthly offers
- Discover new series available to you
- Browse the Bonus Bucks catalog
- Share your feedback

Visit us at:
ReaderService.com

RSI3